DOCTOR WHO

73 YARDS

73 YARDS

Based on the BBC television adventure
by Russell T Davies

SCOTT HANDCOCK

BOOKS

2

BBC Books, an imprint of Ebury Publishing
20 Vauxhall Bridge Road
London SW1V 2SA

BBC Books is part of the Penguin Random House group of companies whose
addresses can be found at global.penguinrandomhouse.com

Doctor Who is produced in Wales by Bad Wolf
with BBC Studios Productions.

Executive Producers: Russell T Davies, Julie Gardner,
Jane Tranter, Joel Collins & Phil Collinson

First published by BBC Books in 2024

www.penguin.co.uk

A CIP catalogue record for this book is available from the British Library

ISBN 9781785948862

Editorial Director: Albert DePetrillo
Project Editor: Steve Cole
Cover Design: Two Associates
Cover illustration: Dan Liles

Typeset by Rocket Editorial Ltd

Printed and bound in Great Britain by Clays Ltd, Elcograf S.p.A.

The authorised representative in the EEA is Penguin Random House Ireland,
Morrison Chambers, 32 Nassau Street, Dublin D02 YH68

Contents

Chapter 1	The Land and the Sea	1
Chapter 2	The Hiker	15
Chapter 3	Y Pren Marw	23
Chapter 4	Mad Jack	39
Chapter 5	Glyngatwyg	49
Chapter 6	Carla	59
Chapter 7	Kate	75
Chapter 8	Ruby	93
Chapter 9	Roger	109
Chapter 10	Marti	117
Chapter 11	Cardiff	123
Chapter 12	The Aftermath	143
Chapter 13	The TARDIS	149
Chapter 14	The Woman	157
Chapter 15	The End	165

For Alfred and Bella…
One day, your mum might let you read this.

Also, for Mum…
Who might read this, one day.

And for Nan…
Who would have been chuffed.

Chapter 1
The Land and the Sea

9 November 2024

It was another brisk, autumnal morning on the west coast of Wales. Imposing limestone cliffs stood defiant against the waves, as they had done for thousands upon thousands of years; they stood tall above the sea, the victim of its eternal push and pull, while their vertical pocks and grooves made it look like they were reaching for the stars.

An orange sun crept out above a vast and endless horizon, peering up to join them. As the freezing waters slammed against the rocks, and a harsh wind buffeted the hiking trails beyond, it offered a misguided promise of warmth.

On the edge of the highest clifftop, the sounds of the sea were drowned out by an even more ancient sound:

the curious mechanical wheezing that accompanied the rhythmic materialisation of an old police box.

This was the TARDIS – a sophisticated space-time machine from a long-forgotten world – and, while it seemingly managed not to attract attention wherever it might appear, anywhere in the universe, it never looked quite as out of place as it did in that moment, on the top of a remote Welsh clifftop.

A moment later, the doors to the tall blue box snapped open, and out stepped the Doctor. He wore a warm yellow duffel coat over a tight white-and-blue-striped top, and a pair of reliable jeans; the look was then capped off with a simple red beanie on his head. If there was any doubt that he'd been anticipating their current location, his opening exclamation confirmed it.

'Yes!' the Doctor grinned. 'Spectacular! We are in Wales!'

'How can you tell?' His best friend Ruby Sunday followed him outside, closing the TARDIS door behind her. She braced herself against the icy coastal air. Unlike the Doctor, she was a little less certain about where they might have materialised. She'd had enough time to grab a jacket, pulling it on over a cosy orange jumper, but her checked skirt and leggings immediately felt like a very bad decision.

The Doctor breathed in deeply, enjoying every hit of the salty air.

'That smell,' he sighed contentedly. He gestured to their surroundings. 'That green. That coastline, Ruby!'

Ruby followed his gaze, savouring the serenity. It was a far cry from a world like Kastarion 3. There, they'd emerged from the TARDIS straight onto a battlefield where the sky was thick with fog and stank of smoke. Here, however, everything seemed so fresh: a tiny little corner of Earth, her own small planet, billions of years old, and yet it still felt completely new, as if mankind had yet to discover it.

Ahead of them, she could see miles of bleak countryside, extending into farmland further out. A single, barren tree appeared to have survived the elements, standing stark against the skyline. Its branches had been blasted by the fiercest of coastal winds over a great many decades, giving it the appearance of an umbrella that had been turned inside-out.

Then there was the sea – that majestic, infinite sea – stretching out far into the distance behind them. The only things that suggested its scale were a couple of distant islands. It made Ruby feel so small. People had always said there was so much of Earth we still don't know about, entire worlds and ecosystems hidden

3

beneath the waves. Was this how the universe felt to the Doctor? On the surface, it all seemed so simple. But then, when you stopped to consider it – all the currents and tides and depths, constantly changing – there was always something new to explore.

'The rocks and the water, it never ends!' the Doctor cheered. 'The war between the land and the sea.'

Ruby followed as he marched away towards the farmland, negotiating the soft and spongy ground. She thought about where they were. She was so close to home.

'I've been to Wales twice,' she said, trying her best to maintain her footing. 'I went to see Shygirl in Cardiff. Then I went to the Mumbles, when I was 16, because of a boy. I think I broke his heart, but there you go.'

'Oh, bless him,' replied the Doctor. 'Mind you, Roger ap Gwilliam. That's a bad example of the Welsh. Terrifying!' He clapped his hands to reinforce the point. 'The most dangerous Prime Minister in history. He led the world to the brink of nuclear ...' He paused. 'What year are you from?'

'2024.'

'Ooh, ha ha. Yikes. He's 2046. Spoilers! Forget I said anything!' He picked up his pace, knowing that Ruby wouldn't let him end it there.

'No, no, tell me what happened!' she insisted. But they were interrupted by a sudden crump and the faintest metallic chime. Both of them looked to the ground.

'Oh, no no no, what's this?' The Doctor lifted his boot. It had snagged on a strand of cotton, part of a far more intricate design almost seven feet in diameter, not unlike an oversized cobweb.

The Doctor crouched down to inspect it more closely. 'Oh, it's a circle,' he realised.

He followed the pattern round. Strings of thread looped and intersected, supported by twigs and wire, all beautifully intertwined. Some of the threads had trinkets hanging from them – tiny keepsakes and mementoes – ranging from a doll's head to silver toy shoes, love hearts to clothes pegs; others hugged to tiny, rolled-up scrolls containing messages; one even had a chain of bird skulls dangling from it.

'Someone made this,' said the Doctor reverentially, picking up a sprig of dried flowers. 'Sorry, man, sorry. I'm sorry.'

'It's like something made by children,' Ruby added, kneeling beside him. 'Lucky charms and bird skulls. There are messages, look!'

She unfurled one of the scrolls from its thread and

opened it up. The ink had started to bleed into the paper but she could still make it out.

'*I miss you,*' she read. 'That's all it says.' She opened another. '*Rest in peace, Mad Jack.*' She paused, realising what they must have stumbled into. 'Oh, poor old Mad Jack, bless him. It must be some sort of memorial.'

The Doctor didn't reply. If he had chosen that moment to say something, an unearthly gust of wind had swallowed his words. Ruby turned to face him…

But the Doctor was suddenly nowhere to be seen.

'I said it's like a memorial!' Ruby yelled, trying to get his attention.

But again, the Doctor didn't reply. He must have gone back to the TARDIS, she supposed.

'All right,' sighed Ruby, getting to her feet, 'don't be doing that to me!' She strode over to the TARDIS and tried the door. It wouldn't budge. Even her key refused to open it.

'It's locked,' shouted Ruby, calling up at the TARDIS windows. Was it just her imagination, or did they seem darker than usual? 'You've locked it from the inside. Can you hear me?' Then a new thought struck her: a reason why the Doctor might have snuck away without saying. 'I hope you're not having a pee round the back…'

With just the right level of warning, she ventured round to the back of the TARDIS. But her relief at being wrong was swapped out for a growing sense of dread. If the Doctor wasn't here or inside the TARDIS, where was he?

She stumbled back to the front of the TARDIS instead. In his distinctive yellow duffel coat, she was bound to spot him somewhere, even if he had wandered off without her. But no, there was still no sign. Just miles of sea and rolling countryside and ...

Wait, was that someone else out there with them?

Ruby squinted. Some distance away was a figure. Not the Doctor – he'd have stood out like a beacon – but someone new. Someone who hadn't been there when they'd first landed.

It looked like a woman with long white hair – an old woman, perhaps? – dressed in black, standing merrily where she was. She seemed to be staring at Ruby. But then, Ruby was also staring at her.

Had they been trespassing, Ruby wondered?

But the stranger didn't seem to be angry. She wasn't advancing or raising her voice. Instead, she just stood there, watching. Her head tilted conversationally from side to side. Was this stranger talking to someone? If she was, there was no one else out there.

No one but Ruby.

Ruby took her chance. 'Hello!' she cried out loudly, yelling above the wind. 'Have you seen my friend? He was here! He's um...'

But the woman didn't seem to be listening. She just stood there, watching Ruby, wringing her hands in a pattern, over and over. Now and then, she would shrug, almost like an apology – no, not quite an apology, more like: *sorry, it can't be helped* – and the longer Ruby met her gaze, the more she noticed the pattern... and the more unnerved she became.

She called out, one more time. 'Doctor? Where are you? Doctor!'

But still no reply. Just the wind, the sea and the woman's silent words.

Desperate, Ruby hurried back to the TARDIS, giving the doors her hardest shove.

'Doctor!' she shouted, banging at them both with her fist. When she got no answer, she rested her head next to the keyhole and whispered, 'Doctor? Are you there?'

Then she realised that the TARDIS was different.

Previously, it had possessed some kind of aura, inviting people like Ruby towards it – a mysterious, timeless warmth, accompanied by a soft, reassuring hum. But now, the blue box was silent, still and cold. Even the lamplight on the top of its roof had faded to nothing.

'You're dead,' she told the TARDIS. 'Are you dead?'

The TARDIS, like the absent Doctor, didn't reply. Ruby gave it the benefit of the doubt and held her ear against the wood, hoping to hear the faintest hum or clunk or groan ... but nothing happened.

Ruby was all alone – well, almost alone. She turned back to the woman. 'Sorry! I want to ask,' she started, then it occurred to her that the woman still couldn't hear her. 'Hold on!' she yelled, hurrying forward a couple of steps, before having to stop to correct her footing on the uneven ground.

When she looked back up, however, she didn't seem to have made any progress. She wasn't any closer to the woman. In fact, somehow, the woman appeared to have changed location and yet remained in the exact same pose: framed against the dull grey sky, rubbing her palms and shrugging.

Right, Ruby thought. *That's weird.* 'Could you just wait there?'

Ruby ran a few more feet, picking up her pace to catch up with the motionless bystander. Then, when Ruby stopped ... could it be?

The woman seemed even further away.

No, not further away – *the same distance away*, at least, relative to Ruby. But now the woman stood behind a rock when she hadn't before.

Surely Ruby would have seen her move, though? No one could hop about like this so quickly, never mind an old woman out in the cold. And yet the woman never actually appeared to move while Ruby was looking at her. Instead, she simply stood, fixed in that same position, repeating her already familiar gestures.

'Okay.' Ruby accepted the challenge and ran forward another ten feet. She was determined to catch the stranger out this time. But when she looked up …

The woman remained the same distance from her, and yet further back still, this time framed beneath the canopy of the leafless old tree.

Ruby paused. Who was this woman watching her? The white hair made her seem old and yet she moved with such speed. And who had time for games like this anyway? Ruby had made it clear she was looking for help.

She noticed that the woman was dressed in a long black smock. Perhaps some kind of mourning dress? Maybe that's why the woman was up here, to visit the memorial (if that's what it was)? There was something unnerving about her too, as though the fabric of that dress was stealing all the light around her – like stepping into a darkened room on a sunny day. The contrast was startling.

'Okay, very clever!' congratulated Ruby at the top of her voice. 'Are you part of this? Where's the Doctor? What have you done to him?'

Whatever the woman was saying, Ruby wished she could hear her. It seemed to be the same thing she'd been saying before, with the same practised signals. But what was she saying, and how was she saying it? Ruby couldn't make out any expression. Was she smiling, solemn, angry? A combination of the above? From where Ruby now stood, the woman's face was just a shape, haloed beneath a thatch of long white hair.

And yet, there was something not quite right about that face … It seemed a little too round, too white – a deathly white, white as chalk – and … was that some kind of curve across her cheek? It only seemed to affect the left side of her face, creasing up from mouth to eyelid. A scar, perhaps?

Shaking away the thought, Ruby had an idea. She pulled out her phone, unlocked it and aimed it at the woman like a weapon. She zoomed the camera lens in, as close as she could, and—

Snap!

Ruby took a photo. Then another, followed by another, just to make certain. From this far away, the woman's face was still obscured, but she was sure that if she zoomed in ...

No. Ruby was wrong. The face was still little more than a blur, an assortment of pixels. Worse, the environment around the woman seemed unaffected. Almost like she didn't want to be seen.

Ruby lowered her phone and looked up at the stranger. Desperation was taking hold now.

'Can you help me?' she asked, her voice tinged with fear. 'Please?'

But the woman didn't answer ... or if she did, the answer hadn't changed. Those same repeated motions: the rubbing of palms, the shrugging.

Over and over. On and on.

An hour passed. Ruby was sitting on the cold wet grass by the TARDIS. Her clothes were now sodden from dew and spray from the sea, but that didn't matter. All that mattered was finding the Doctor. He had to be around here somewhere.

She kept thinking through what had happened to them, hunting for clues. Perhaps he'd mentioned something significant that drew him away? Even in that shortest amount of time, they'd said so much.

Shygirl.

The Mumbles.

Mad Jack (rest in peace).

The war between the land and the sea.

Roger William… something?

Ruby repeated these phrases over like a mantra, trying to ignore the distant woman. But she knew that if she looked up, even for a second, the woman would be there watching her…

Waiting.

Another hour passed, followed by another and then another. As the sun drifted slowly across the sky and a cold wind battered the TARDIS, Ruby checked her phone. Time was marching on and her battery was failing.

It was time to take action.

With effort, she rose to her feet and crossed to the TARDIS.

'I'm starving and freezing.' Ruby shivered. 'I can't stay out here all night. But I'll come back, I promise. My phone says it's November the 9th, 2024, so … stay on November the 9th, okay? Don't go without me.'

This put her in mind of Ashleigh, an old friend from Tameside. No matter how clearly you told her where you'd be or when to meet, she'd always go storming off somewhere else without letting you know. Ruby had lost so many Saturdays afternoons tracking her down.

'Oh, and this is really rude, okay?' she added, giving the TARDIS a playful kick.

It still didn't respond.

So, Ruby turned her back on TARDIS and woman alike and started to walk. Embarking on the longest journey of her life.

Chapter 2
The Hiker

As the long afternoon drew on, Ruby folded her arms across her chest and braced herself against the increasing autumn cold. It began to grow steadily darker, and she could see lights on the horizon – a simple, quaint Welsh village enticing her to find someplace warm. And every time she glanced back over her shoulder, the mysterious woman was there, gesturing: always the exact same distance and movement. Never catching up, never standing still.

Ruby tried counting the seconds before looking back, in case that might help her catch her stalker unawares.

But it never did.

The woman never seemed to actually move. She simply remained in the same, repeated pose, as the wind whipped up around them.

At one point, Ruby saw a bird – perhaps a kite or gull – fly up towards the cliffs before pulling away, seemingly as spooked as she was.

Faster now, Ruby kept moving. She reached the crest of a hill, skidding down the mud on the other side before spinning to look back up at the ridge…

The woman wasn't there for once, not yet. Maybe if Ruby waited, she could catch her on the approach. She'd be close enough to confront her now – and whether the woman was following her or not, Ruby couldn't deny a sense of relief at no longer seeing her.

Deciding not to tempt fate any further, Ruby chose instead to continue her journey towards the tiny village on the horizon. But as she turned, a visceral shiver ran down her spine, a terrible chill so much colder than the weather around her.

Because there was the woman standing, impossibly, *ahead* of her. But how? She was still the same distance away, so it seemed, but she'd somehow managed to shift her entire location. The terrain was hardly easy to navigate, Ruby knew that much, and there was no sense of the woman having hurried or catching her breath. If anything, she remained absolutely still, as if she had *always* been there, gesturing away like it was the most normal thing in the world.

That apologetic shrug, again and again. But apologising for what?

With the light now fading faster, Ruby raced along the coastal path, high above the waves, as quickly as she was able. The ferocious winds buffeted her, and she was acutely aware of just how easily she could lose her footing. She was afraid of falling, of course, but knew to keep her distance from the edge. Just as this woman kept her distance from Ruby.

There was precious little light left either. The final embers of sun were beginning to dip beneath the horizon, just as delicate flakes of snow began to fall. Normally, Ruby would find comfort in this. There was a magic to snow, she thought; she'd loved it all her life. It had been there on the day she was born. And yet here, in that moment, it seemed somehow unwelcoming... like someone holding your coat as they show you the door.

Ruby looked up to face the woman again. It wasn't the sort of place to be out on your own, not at this time of day, and certainly not at her age – assuming the woman was as old as she looked? Ruby couldn't quite tell from this distance.

Ruby shivered again as a sudden voice shocked her. 'Hello there!'

She spun round. To her relief, there was someone else marching towards her – a woman who was, thankfully, getting closer – dressed in a pastel-blue cagoule with sturdy hiking boots, supported by a pair of Nordic trekking poles. She was probably middle-aged, Ruby guessed, more than a little jolly and apparently ready for anything.

'You must be mad,' the hiker told Ruby, looking her outfit up and down. 'Is that all you're wearing?'

'Yeah, I got kind of … caught?' Ruby replied, making it all up on the spot. (The Doctor seemed to make this look so easy.) 'Um. The car broke down?'

'Oh no! You poor thing!'

'I know,' Ruby agreed. 'Bit of a day.' Then she pointed towards the village the hiker had come from. 'What's that, down there? Where is it?'

The hiker checked over her shoulder just to make sure of herself. 'Oh, that's *Glyngatwyg*,' she answered, overemphasising every syllable, 'if you'll forgive my pronunciation … which they don't!' She offered a gentle chuckle to lighten the mood. 'I think they've got a garage. Where's the car?'

Ah yes, this was the tricky bit: the broken-down car that most definitely wasn't a complex space-time machine disguised as a defunct police box.

'Um, it's just, that way,' Ruby suggested, glancing behind her, 'but…' Her voice trailed off. Suddenly, this hiker in the middle of nowhere seemed really familiar. 'I haven't met you before, have I?'

'I don't think so,' said the hiker, a little uncertain. 'Have you?'

'No. Just, that was a different…' *A different planet?* Ruby brushed the thought away. She was lost in the middle of nowhere – no Doctor, no TARDIS – her imagination running away with her, making random connections.

The hiker was a comforting presence, she decided, before leaning in conspiratorially. 'That woman, over there…' Ruby pointed out the distant apparition. 'Can you see her?'

'Course I can,' nodded the hiker. 'Who is she?'

'She's, um…' How best to put this? 'This is going to sound a bit mad, but she's following me. I think I trespassed or something. Could you tell her I'm sorry?'

'Sorry for what?'

'Well… I don't know.'

The hiker looked at Ruby, then the woman just a short walk beyond her. 'Have I walked into something…?' Her once warm tone was replaced by one of suspicion.

'No no no, sorry,' said Ruby, quickly, 'but look, you're going that way. So. Could you just tell her? I'm fine. And she can go home?'

'I'm intrigued now!' The hiker smiled again, seemingly satisfied. 'And it's no skin off my nose. But once that's done, get in the warm, both of you, whatever little game this is.'

'Of course.' Ruby nodded, like it was her absolute top priority. Then she watched as the hiker strode merrily past her, towards the mysterious woman on the horizon. To her simultaneous relief and surprise, the woman remained where she was standing as the hiker approached. She didn't hop back and forth in the blink of an eye; she simply stayed…

Meaning the hiker was getting closer…

Leading to answers… or an ending.

'And could you ask her,' Ruby added, crying out, 'if she knows the Doctor?'

The hiker spun round, concerned. 'D'you need a doctor?' She was ready to dig out her first aid kit without a moment's hesitation.

'No, it's just…' Ruby gave up trying to come up with clever excuses. 'Could you ask?'

The hiker beamed. 'I'll try!' And she continued her walk.

It must have taken all of a minute for the hiker to reach the woman, even over the difficult terrain. Ruby watched and waited, each and every second feeling longer than the one that came before it. She just wanted to understand. Why was this happening? What had she done wrong? And why had the Doctor abandoned her like this?

Curiously, the woman never dropped her gaze, even when the hiker was clearly addressing her. Ruby couldn't make out what either was saying, but she found this behaviour uncomfortable: the manner in which the woman refused to stop staring, even now there was someone new – someone friendly and chatty – standing right next to her.

There was a new heaviness to the air. Now the hiker also turned to face Ruby – but there was a stiffness to the move, like she couldn't quite bring herself to look at the girl she'd left behind. It was hard to make out from this distance, but was that a look of horror? Was the hiker afraid of her?

As if in answer to that question, the hiker backed away with a terrible shriek. Then she ran – all the while, keeping both eyes locked on Ruby for fear that she might ... what?

What did she think that Ruby might do to her?

Was it something the woman had said? That inexplicable woman who wouldn't stop staring and shrugging.

Ruby realised she didn't want to discover the answer. Instead, she turned and ran towards Glyngatwyg, as a peal of distant thunder threatened to follow … and the woman with it.

Chapter 3
Y Pren Marw

As Ruby's journey grew longer, her pace became slower. The snowfall wasn't heavy but it was persistent, dusting the surrounding countryside with a delicate sprinkle of winter. It shone beneath the dusky moonlight, causing the strange, unfamiliar landscape to glow. Frightened and alone, Ruby could almost believe the snow was mocking her, delighting in revealing how much further she had to walk.

For an hour, it seemed her expedition would never end. Step after countless step, her feet were cold and damp, icy snowflakes soaked into her collar, and her ragged breath formed misty clouds in front of her face.

She allowed herself a laugh, albeit a nervous one, when a familiar high-pitched shriek caught her off-guard, followed by a trio of short explosions. There were fireworks somewhere nearby – the final flurry in the weekend after Guy Fawkes Night – screaming high into the cold night sky. Each one made Ruby jump for the slightest of seconds, before giving way to a sensation of relief. It meant she was getting closer to civilisation.

Noisy civilisation.

After twenty more minutes of trekking, she found herself on tarmac: a proper road (rather than a dirt track) into the village. It wasn't long before she came across an older man walking his dog. He wore a scarf and thick, black overcoat, and even his spaniel sported a fetching cable knit sweater. Ruby couldn't help but envy both.

'Excuse me!' she called, trying to catch the man's attention, but he continued his walk without so much as a glance. Only the dog seemed to notice. 'Sorry, but can you help me? It's my … car.'

Ruby hurried across the road and ran up to the stranger. He didn't seem one for small talk.

'Garage'll be shut now,' said the man, increasing his pace.

'Yeah, sorry, I'm on my own and lost track of time. I need a place for the night.'

'Can't help you there,' the dog walker told her quickly.

'No, but there must be somewhere,' Ruby insisted. 'Like a hotel or B&B or something?'

The old man slowed to a halt and finally faced her. If he'd been paying her more attention, he might have registered the other stranger a little way off, standing comfortably (impossibly) on top of a cattle grid.

'You could always try Y Pren Marw,' he suggested.

Ruby looked at him quizzically. 'What's that?' she asked.

'Y Pren Marw,' he repeated more slowly.

'Apron what?' Ruby tried to ape the pronunciation.

The old man smiled with gloomy relish. 'In English, it means: the Dead Tree.' Then he tugged on the spaniel's lead and strode away.

Ruby followed the road and old-fashioned lampposts into the village, pursued by the weirdest stalker in the world. Whenever she checked back over her shoulder, the woman was there. Sometimes, although there was no way anyone could cover such distance so quickly, the woman even appeared ahead of her, as if leading the way.

Eventually, Ruby reached the foot of a gentle hill.

To her left, she passed an old cemetery; headstones peered over the top of a drystone wall, as if to observe her.

Further up the slope, obscured by drizzle, Ruby could just about make out a sign, swinging on its hinges in the wind. It depicted an ancient tree blasted by the elements, overshadowed by three simple, faded words in blood-red paint:

Y Pren Marw.

The Dead Tree, Ruby realised, approaching the building.

It was a pub, of course. The sign declared, proudly or otherwise, that it had been established there since 1863 and – despite a few modern concessions such as a phone-box-turned-defibrillator and some strings of outdoor lighting – the whole place felt like something from an old-fashioned horror film. And yet, as she crunched up the gravel towards it, she saw a golden glow beyond the windows. There were lights on, people inside ... maybe even a fire?

Finally, Ruby thought, a warm welcome.

The entire pub fell silent as Ruby entered.

Okay then. *Not* so warm a welcome.

On that night, Y Pren Marw's contingent consisted of five locals scattered about its main parlour – or at least, the half that was situated closest to the fire. The room itself was, in some ways, beautiful: lots of ornate beams and wood, decorated with love spoons and horseshoes and brass, all built around that traditional open fireplace. But, for all the cosy trappings, the atmosphere was stagnant. There was more than a hint of damp in the air, a coolness to the walls that reminded Ruby, randomly, of her old school History trips. If Y Pren Marw had been established in 1863, it felt as if little had changed... except perhaps for the large TV that hung from a bracket on the wall by the fire.

It was showing a game of football. The crowd went wild as somebody scored but no one in that room seemed to care. Was anyone watching?

Right now, the answer was no – all eyes were on Ruby.

'State on you,' sneered one of them: a woman in her fifties, daubed in tattoos, worn out by a lifetime of work and hard as nails. She turned to an older lady, sat by the bar in a smart red beret. 'Who goes out in this without a coat?'

The old woman smiled her most noncommittal smile as Ruby moved forward.

'No, I've ... lost my things,' said Ruby apologetically, not that she really had anything to apologise for. 'Sorry, it's kind of a long story.'

'Is it?' the first woman asked in a tone that made it very clear it shouldn't be.

'Yeah. My name's Ruby, by the way...' If she expected an introduction, it never came. Ruby hoped the owner might be more hospitable... until that same hard-bitten woman took her place behind the bar and Ruby realised: she *was* the owner.

Lowri Palin had inherited Y Pren Marw when she was 38 years old, twice the age of the young girl now standing opposite her. Along with the building, she had also inherited a lot of its regular clientele, including the old woman, Enid Meadows, and Lowri's oldest friend, Joshua Steele. Others from the village occasionally wandered in, but you could depend on Enid and Joshua sitting there, night after night.

More recently, a couple of teenagers, Ifor and Lucy, had decided to make the pub their regular haunt – a decision that Lowri was fine with on the proviso they kept themselves very much to themselves... which they did.

Now she had another one to deal with. At least, Lowri guessed that this Ruby was roughly late teens. She had an air of confidence, if not experience, and clearly hadn't planned for the local weather. Lowri almost felt sorry for her.

'I don't suppose...' Ruby stammered, shaking off

the cold. I'm a bit stuck. Have you got a room for the night?'

'I have. For 65 quid,' replied Lowri. 'I haven't got anything in for breakfast but I can do toast and yoghurt.'

'Don't let her cook, for god's sake!' urged Josh from his seat by the fire.

'Shut it,' snapped Lowri.

'Don't let her cook!' he warned again with the cheekiest smile.

Joshua Steele was about eight years younger than Lowri. They'd known each another for decades, ever since they were teenagers themselves. Friends at school always joked they were soulmates. Then friends in the village, as they all grew older, used to say the same. Everyone saw their potential, except Lowri and Joshua, who had always struggled to maintain that they were 'just good butts'…

At least until they'd had a few drinks at a summer wedding, 17 years ago, and Lowri decided to have 'the chat'.

It was a conversation they'd both known was coming, one they'd desperately hoped to avoid, but too many toasts to the happy couple inspired the pair to acknowledge the truth. They were good friends, yes, but there was a deeper love there too: an attraction that they'd tried to deny for so many years.

They'd shared a kiss that night, the best kiss that either of them could ever remember. But that was all that became of their feelings. It wouldn't be right, Josh told her, not with the wedding – *his* wedding. Perhaps if they'd spoken sooner?

Lowri had lived with those words for 17 years; she'd lived with him coming into her family's pub, day after day (any excuse to see her, everyone knew it); and now she put up with him warning strangers off cooked breakfasts she wasn't even offering – not that the newcomer seemed to mind.

'No, that's fine,' said Ruby, checking her pockets. 'But I haven't got any cash. Can I pay with my phone?'

'Can you what?' Lowri looked at her like she was speaking an alien language.

'Can I pay? With my phone?'

'Pay with your *phone*?'

'Yeah.'

Lowri looked to the others. 'How do you pay? With your phone?' Her voice was full of caution.

'Oh, well, it's like ...' Ruby faltered, as if considering how best to explain. 'It's sort of online banking, but the phone can transfer money from my account to—'

Lowri slammed a portable Wi-Fi card reader onto the bar, pushing it forward. 'Yes, you can pay with your phone,' she confirmed disdainfully, entering the correct amount on the screen before sliding it over.

Ruby fumbled with her phone, avoiding eye contact. She wanted nothing more than for the ground to swallow her up. The last thing she'd intended was to cause offence. 'Sorry,' she blurted, pressing her phone against the reader, followed by a quieter 'Thank you' as it chimed its receipt.

Lowri said nothing. She just took the device away and went back to her work.

Enid Meadows had been sizing Ruby up from her bar-side stool. Now late into her seventies, she frequented Y Pren Marw to continue her studies in quiet contemplation. Tonight, she was translating the poetry of Catullus for the umpteenth time. It was a hobby of hers: using her passion for words and language to evoke long-lost romances, despite never once allowing herself to find the same. She'd known men throughout her life, of course – good men, too – but in the eyes of Enid Meadows, not one could hold a candle to academia.

Now life had passed her by.

All she had to her name was a tiny cottage, filled as much with rot as it was with books. In the pub, she had a stool at the bar for as long as she wanted, though she wasn't one for company – she never bothered to take off her coat, and the locals all knew that she was 'only staying for one' (even if that 'one' could last an evening).

They also knew it didn't take much to prick her ears.

'We're not quite the Dark Ages, young lady,' Enid said, turning to Ruby. 'Despite what they say.'

'Apparently, next week, we're getting Christianity!' cheered Joshua, raising his glass.

'Throw them to the lions!' roared Ifor, sat in his corner with Lucy. He wore a tight leather jacket and sported an array of piercings and eyeliner. She wore an unimpressed expression and a chequered shirt.

Ifor looked up from his phone with the wettest grin. 'Throw them to the lions and watch them getting eaten alive! With great big teeth an' blood an' things!'

Lucy narrowed her eyes at Ruby, burning with resentment. Enid recognised the signs. Lucy hated Ifor in that moment, simply for daring to pay Ruby more attention than he'd ever give to her. It was classic unrequited love. Lucy had told them all about it one night, when Ifor was away in Swansea on a date.

The girl had the most enormous crush on him, had

done since the moment they met. When they were both 16, at a house party, she plucked up the courage to tell him. She confessed her deepest, innermost feelings... and Ifor just laughed. So hard, right in her face. She had to be joking, right?

Only, Lucy hadn't been joking. She loved him. And he said that he loved her, but not in *that way*. Surely she understood? I mean, they'd been friends for so long, she must know him better that that?

Wasn't it obvious?

The rest of the pub all knew, not that they'd comment. Even Ifor couldn't say the words. Not out loud, not even to Lucy. Maybe he hoped to hear them from someone else. Sometimes Enid asked about a girlfriend, hoping that this might prompt a correction. But for as long as he couldn't say it, Lucy lived in hope it wasn't true, and that he might one day grow interested in her.

Right now, however, all Ifor seemed to be interested in was Ruby.

'Drink?' Lowri asked, drumming her fingers on the bar.

'Yes, um, I'll have...' Ruby examined the shelves, not sure what to go for. There was so much choice, and she'd had such a mad day... but she also had to plan and keep a clear head. 'No, I'll just have a coke,' she decided eventually.

'Last of the big spenders,' Lowri sighed, fetching her a watered-down soda.

Ruby crossed to the window while she waited. 'Do you mind if I ask?' she said to nobody in particular. 'There's this woman. Outside. Can you see her?'

She tugged back the curtain, revealing the windswept view beyond. Even through the drizzled glass, that same woman was visible, standing in the storm. The Welsh weather lashed all about her but she remained fixed on her chosen spot. Her only movements: that shrug and the wringing of hands.

Joshua rose to join Ruby. 'She'll be bloody freezing, mun.'

'But d'you know who she is?' Ruby asked.

'Never seen her,' said Josh, squinting through the glass. 'Why, who is she?'

'I don't know.'

Enid didn't even bother looking up from her notebook. 'I rather think, in this sort of weather, you should ask her in,' she declared, pondering her Latin declensions.

'No,' Ruby explained, a little impatiently, 'she's not *with* me. She's just … *following* me.'

Suddenly, this seemed worth Enid putting her pen down. 'What for?' she asked, shifting on her stool for a better view.

'I don't know,' said Ruby again.

'But she's definitely following you?'

'I think so.'

Lowri interrupted their conversation. 'Five quid,' she demanded, shoving a coke in Ruby's direction.

'How much?!' Ruby reluctantly paid with her phone.

'Pardon me for stating the obvious,' said Enid, picking up their previous conversation. 'But if there's a woman following you, have you tried asking her *why*?'

'No,' replied Ruby meekly.

'Oh my god!' Lucy groaned with thinly veiled contempt.

'I'll ask her now,' Josh told them, draining his pint glass. 'I'm off home for my tea! I'll send her in for a pie and a pint, and you can pay on your Magic Phone.' Lowri laughed a little too hard at that. 'Night, girls!'

'Night then, Josh!' Lowri yelled from behind the bar.

'Safely home,' chimed Enid.

As Joshua strode to the door, Ruby hurried over to catch him.

'Could you ask her …?' She paused. How best to

explain this? 'There was a friend of mine, in a yellow duffel coat. Could you ask her if she's seen him? Black guy,' she gestured, 'about five-ten?'

'I'll give it a go!' Josh replied, a little bemused. 'Cheerio then!'

'See you tomorrow, Josh,' Lowri called, like it was a promise. But her voice was lost to the wind and rain as he pulled open the door, heaving it shut behind him. Everyone else went back to what they were doing. Enid translated her poems, Lowri watched the TV, Ifor played on his phone and Lucy pretended not to watch him. Meanwhile, Ruby remained by the window, staring at the woman down the street. She watched as Joshua raised his collar against the cold, trudging steadily closer towards her.

'Following's the wrong word,' Ruby said to whoever was listening, 'cos she doesn't… approach. She comes so far, then it's like she stays away. Never comes any closer.'

Enid looked up from her papers, enjoying a challenge. 'I can't think of a synonym, for keeping your distance,' she mused. 'I suppose, to coin a new word: in Latin, it would be *semperdistans*: always distant. She is *semperdistans* to you.'

Summing it up in a word felt strangely comforting,

Ruby thought, especially a Latin word. It felt like maybe she wasn't the first person this had ever happened to. She turned back to the window just as Joshua reached the woman. Both were silhouetted under a lamppost.

As with the hiker before, the woman kept looking at Ruby as Joshua spoke. Then Ruby saw him pause – he'd asked her his questions and now he was listening, but what was she saying to him? Whatever it was, Ruby felt the air around her grow heavy, watching as Joshua's shoulders tensed and his whole body stiffened. Y Pren Marw's joker was no longer smiling.

Joshua turned to face Ruby, their eyes locking for the briefest of moments through the rain … then with a terrible, guttural scream, he ran swiftly away … away from the woman, away from the pub, and most of all, away from Ruby Sunday.

On hearing the scream, Ifor leapt to his feet, gawping out of the window next to Ruby. 'Oh my god,' he cried. 'Josh is running!'

'That's his wife, shouting, that is,' said Lowri drily.

'Really, though,' Ifor continued, 'he is *running*! He spoke to that woman, and then, he ran away. He ran away like the devil was on his bum!' He turned delightedly to Ruby. 'What did she say to him?'

'I don't know.'

'Who is she?'

'I don't know!'

Ruby's sudden exasperation silenced the room. Only Enid dared break the tension.

'It seems that Josh is *semperdistans*, too,' the old woman smirked, unaware that the man was screaming all the way home.

Chapter 4
Mad Jack

A hundred thoughts raced through Ruby's head. Why was this happening to her? Why now? Why was this woman '*semperdistans*' to her? And what had happened to the Doctor? One moment, he'd been right next to her and the next… gone. Which might be just about plausible if he wasn't one of the most conspicuous people she'd ever met.

Something had happened out there, on the cliffs. Something to do with that memorial, perhaps? She tried to remember anything and everything that could be significant.

'I wonder…' Ruby was thinking aloud now. 'I thought… I was with my friend and … we walked into this thing. Up on the clifftops. Like a circle of cotton and little toy things, like charms, and the skulls of little birds. Almost like a witchcraft sort of thing.'

Ruby stepped into the centre of the room, like a gladiator awaiting their fate in the Colosseum, turning to each of the others for their support. But not one of them offered comfort. Instead, the locals all looked to one another – Lowri, to Enid, to Ifor, to Lucy – and a dark glance passed between them.

The mention of witchcraft seemed to have changed everything.

'What d'you mean, cotton?' asked Lowri, switching off the TV.

There was only the howl of the storm outside now. Even the roar of the fire seemed to fall silent.

'Like ... strands, with these things,' said Ruby, a little unhelpfully.

'Witchcraft is a very strong word,' interjected Enid, closing her notebook. It seemed the diagnosis was terminal. The locals now knew precisely what they were dealing with.

'No, I don't mean it was witchcraft,' Ruby protested. 'I mean it was like ...'

'Where was it?' Lowri demanded.

'Up on the cliff,' replied Ruby, gesturing. 'Couple of miles that way.'

'Bryn Cythraul?' Lowri sounded alarmed now.

'I don't know, was it?'

Ruby looked to the strangers for reassurance, but they offered only dread.

'It's what they call a Fairy Circle,' explained Enid, matter-of-factly.

Lucy sniggered and pointed at Ifor. 'You can ask *him* about that.'

Instantly, Ifor spat back at her – 'Shut your face!' – and Lucy laughed: a vicious, venomous laugh that only Ifor appeared to pick up on.

'When you say you walked into it,' Enid queried, thinking back to the Fairy Circle, 'did you break it?'

'Well. Yes.' Then Ruby sensed a tension fall over the room. 'By mistake,' she added, hoping that might change things. Ifor shook his head. 'But I mean! It's not really magic, is it?'

Enid's voice sank gravely. 'Is it not?'

'I don't think so, no!'

Enid leaned forward. The flames from the guttering fire now cast harsh and eerie shadows across her face. 'The clifftops,' she continued more earnestly, 'are a boundary between the land and the sea. A liminal space, neither here nor there, where rules are suspended.'

The land and the sea. That phrase the Doctor had used. Maybe this was connected after all? Ruby racked her brains.

'And then there's the blood,' declared Lowri.

Ruby whirled round. 'What blood?'

Enid cocked her head, her voice now almost a whisper. 'Do you know why Wales has so many picturesque little castles?'

Ruby shook her head. If she managed to utter a 'no' then nobody heard it.

'They were torture centres, set up by the English.' Enid's voice took on an accusatory tone. 'To rule with fear.'

'Steeped in blood, we are,' added Lowri.

'Tons of blood!' Ifor slavered, and Ruby recoiled.

'This land is a powerful place,' confided Enid. 'It is said that he walks through the gaps: the Spiteful One.'

'No, but it was an accident.' At the back of her mind, Ruby faintly remembered her gran telling her how the legends of Merlin had come from Wales. Did that mean magic was real? 'My friend – he would never disrespect the circle,' she added defensively. 'He'd never do that on purpose. And I walked away when it said, *rest in peace.*'

Lowri's eyes widened in terror. 'What did?'

'One of the little messages, the scrolls.'

Lowri looked at Ruby, appalled. 'You read them?'

'Just a couple.'

'You opened them? And read them?'

Enid picked up on Lowri's anger. 'Why did you do that?'

Ruby couldn't offer a more honest answer than: 'They were there.'

Enid shook her head solemnly. 'I think. Whatever spell was cast in the circle. Is now broken.'

The locals looked to one another, then to Ruby.

'What else did they say?' Lowri asked.

'Just … um …'

'What else did they say?'

'One of them said … *Rest in peace … Mad Jack.*'

As if on cue, the storm clouds rumbled above them, and a sheet of lightning flashed outside the window. The heavens were ganging up on her too.

'Oh my god,' choked Ifor.

'I think, perhaps, that wasn't wise,' Enid added. She had the air of someone breaking bad news as gently as possible.

Ruby kept her cool. 'I thought it was, like, someone's dog, or something?'

'Oh, say that to Mad Jack's face!' Lowri wrung a grubby bar rag in her hands.

'Why, who was he?' A simple question.

A simple answer: 'He was insane.'

43

'And he's *dead*!' asserted a clearly terrified Ifor.

'But now she's broken the circle,' Lowri countered, targeting Ruby.

'Yeah, but what does that *mean*?' Ruby could hear the desperation in Lowri's voice.

Enid took control.

'The charm was very clear,' she told them all calmly. 'Binding his soul to rest. *Semperdistans*, to keep him away.' Then the slightest tremor entered her voice. 'But now you've broken it. And if that woman outside is his herald, that means... Mad Jack is unbound.'

BANG! BANG! BANG!

Three thunderous thumps at the door made everyone jump.

'Oh don't,' Lowri gasped, and Ifor picked up on her horror.

'He'd kill me,' he sobbed, the mascara around his eyes beginning to smear. 'He would kill me. I'm the one he'd kill first, and you know why, don't you!'

Lowri then turned on Ruby. 'What the hell have you done?'

'No,' replied Ruby, rationally, 'that's just someone at the door!'

Three more savage *bangs* suggested anything but.

Lucy started singing. 'Mad Jack, Jack's back!'

'But he'd go home!' Ifor was panicking. 'He wouldn't come here. He'd go home!'

It seemed Lowri had run out of sympathy. 'There's no home to go to, you idiot, not any more!'

'And he would drink,' remembered Enid, 'in this pub.'

'He called this place home.'

Lucy started to giggle. 'He's back, he is! He's back!'

But Ruby stood firmly in front of them. 'That is *not* Mad Jack out there!'

BANG! BANG! BANG!

'Then answer the door!' challenged Lowri.

This had gone far enough now, Ruby convinced herself. She wasn't alone now, nothing could hurt her ... or at least, if it could, it probably wasn't the sort of thing that could be stopped by a simple door, so it would get them all sooner or later. And what was it the Doctor once said to her? *Monsters are just creatures you haven't met yet.* The same was true of Mad Jack ... she hoped.

Steeling herself, just as the Doctor might, Ruby strode to the door of Y Pren Marw, taking the handle tightly in her grasp. She could feel the eyes of the others burning into her – their dread and apprehension was overwhelming.

Her heart was pounding loudly in her chest, louder even than those thumps on the door.

Ruby knew that the longer she left it, the worse it would be; the suspense dragging out, as if she were on a rollercoaster climbing vertically towards the long fall. But she just had to twist the handle and pull it towards her, that's all. Then this would all be over.

With a deep breath, she closed her eyes and twisted the handle, just as a sudden surge of wind blasted the door in, forcing her backwards…

And revealing a man in a smart white apron, struggling with a tray of frozen pasties.

'Hurry up,' the newcomer grumbled, 'I've got my hands full here!'

The accompanying cacophony of laughter told Ruby this was definitely not Mad Jack. She turned to see them all laughing, doubled over in fits of mocking tears – even gentle old Enid Meadows.

It had all been one cruel joke.

'You've got enough pasties for two weeks,' announced the man, barging his way past Ruby. 'Get 'em in the freezer, fast as you can.' He dumped the tray on the counter and realised: 'What's so funny?'

'Her face!' Lowri whooped between laughs. 'Oh my god, her face!'

Ruby confronted the room. She had never felt as unwelcome anywhere as she did in that moment.

'Best one yet, that was!' cheered Ifor, catching his breath before turning to Enid. 'His herald: I loved that bit!'

'Oh my god, that was funny,' said Lowri, wiping tears of laughter from her eyes.

Enid looked Ruby directly in the eye. 'It's racist, my dear, to be blunt; people come from outside, they think we're all witches and druids. For god's sake, child, you walked into a bit of string!' She turned to the man with the pasties. 'Let me stand you a pint, Eddie.'

'Don't mind if I do,' Eddie answered, grabbing a bar stool. Then they were laughing all over again, Lowri switched the TV on and it was business as usual.

Ruby crossed to the open door and stepped back outside. She wasn't sure which was more inhospitable: inside or out? Either way, she needed some air. But as she looked out across the village, down the street, that inscrutable woman remained.

Sorry, she seemed to shrug, again and again. *Sorry*.

Ruby decided it wasn't the time and shut the door ...

If only out of sight meant out of mind.

Chapter 5
Glyngatwyg

Ruby didn't sleep much, that first night. Her mind was full of thoughts of the Doctor and the Woman (as Ruby had come to think of her) and the strangers who had welcomed her so reluctantly into their pub.

The guest room Lowri gave her was small and felt decidedly unused. The heater hadn't been on in months and the sheets smelled distinctly of dust. It didn't come with a key, and Ruby felt awful when she had to wake Lowri the following morning to ask for a bath towel. Her host feigned a polite, happy-to-help smile, leaving Ruby no choice but to imagine what she was actually thinking.

Now, in the cold light of day, Ruby sat alone at the corner table, monitoring the Woman beyond the window. It was like she hadn't moved an inch all night. She stood in exactly the same position she had twelve hours ago. Did she step aside for a passing car, or was she fixed like some kind of monument?

Ruby stirred an all-too-solid splodge of jam into a cheap pot of yoghurt and winced. So much for the most important meal of the day. She added an extra spoonful of sugar to her tea to make up for it.

'Got those spare,' huffed Lowri, throwing down a couple of T-shirts. Each was drably coloured and far too large, but Ruby was grateful for the moment of kindness. 'I'll have them back, mind,' Lowri warned her, storming away again.

No danger there, thought Ruby, nodding her most well-practised 'thank you'.

And still, through the window, the Woman dressed in black continued her pantomime.

One tub of yoghurt and cup of tea later, Ruby had a plan. She decided that she'd go back to the TARDIS and wait for a while, just in case the Doctor went back there. Maybe whatever this was had something to do with the turn of the Earth, and if she waited one 24-hour cycle, the Doctor would blip back into existence and they could be on their way?

She didn't want to worry her mother just yet. She had enough money in her account for a night or two more. So she borrowed a spare phone charger from Lowri, and asked where Ifor lived.

Ifor's mother was surprised to see Ruby when she answered the door – a girl from out of town, visiting Ifor? – but she was welcomed inside and shown up to his room nonetheless: something he claimed Lucy would have a fit about later that evening.

Ifor, however, was thrilled to see Ruby. Last night, he claimed, was the most exciting thing that had happened in Glyngatwyg for decades. 'A stranger arrives from nowhere, in a storm, as darkness falls!' He was enjoying this, Ruby thought – which was useful because she needed someone's help.

When they learned she was off to the clifftops, Ifor's mother offered Ruby a bright yellow canvas camping chair ('for as long as you need') which folded up neatly under Ruby's arm. She carried it all the way back to the TARDIS – its police box shell still outlined incongruously on the horizon – then made herself as comfortable as possible. She deliberately faced the TARDIS, gazing out to sea, knowing that the Woman had no choice but to keep watch behind her, safe on land.

Was she waiting for the Doctor too? Was that why she was following her?

Ruby sat there wondering, long into the afternoon, running through their last exchange the day before. She stayed with the TARDIS for hours, keeping it company, hoping for the Doctor to come back to them.

Soon enough, though, the sun began to set, the cold sea winds whipped up and Ruby felt her fingers losing sensation. She was determined to stay for as long as possible – it was what the Doctor would do, and she couldn't let him down – but eventually the elements got the better of her.

Folding up the brightly coloured camping chair, she told herself she'd try again tomorrow.

That night, Ruby noticed Y Pren Marw was decidedly quieter. Ifor and Lucy sat in their corner, with Enid perched on her stool and Lowri working the bar… but there was no sign of Joshua, arguably the chattiest of their number. Ruby had claimed his table by the fire (it had the best view) until Lowri moved her over to the one by the window. For as long as she drew breath in that pub, Lowri said, nobody was taking Josh's place there…

But still he didn't arrive.

Next morning, Ruby sat in her space by the window, working through breakfast. She crunched on a slab of burnt toast (they'd run out of yoghurt) and sipped the weakest slug of tea from the least-chipped mug.

Nothing seemed to change in Glyngatwyg. Least of all the Woman down the road.

Ruby heard Lowri charging up behind her.

'I said to Josh,' began Lowri calmly, keeping things civil, 'I said, we haven't seen you, he said, I'm never coming back, I said, why, and he said, ask her. So I'm asking you. *Why?*'

Ruby pointed at the Woman down the hill. 'I think he meant, ask *her*.'

Lowri was having none of it. 'Well, I made it very clear to Josh,' she said, making it equally clear to Ruby. 'You will be packing and going. And we won't see you again, as of today. Is that understood?'

She didn't bother to wait for Ruby's answer. Taking one final glance through the window, she felt her blood run cold and hurried back behind her bar as quickly as possible.

There had been rumours about the pub when Lowri first bought it. With a dark past and several deaths, locals claimed it was haunted. But the thought of ghosts or bumps in the night had never once spooked Lowri.

It was only now – confronted by a girl from England with her whole life ahead of her – that Lowri Palin felt truly afraid.

When Ruby came to settle the bill, Lowri couldn't look her in the eye. Neither of them uttered a word. The note that Ruby wrote to say thank you went straight on the fire, and the spare tops she left on the bed went into the bin. As far as Lowri was now concerned, they'd never had a guest called Ruby at Y Pren Marw.

And yet, despite Lowri's best efforts to persuade him, Joshua Steele never returned to his seat by the fire.

As Ruby trekked up to the TARDIS one last time, she decided to phone her mum back in London. She'd held off for as long as possible so as not to concern her, but now seemed as good a time as any.

'You've been there for *how long*?' Carla shrieked. 'I can look into train times. Where are you exactly? Have you got enough money because I can transfer some over on the app. It's instant, these days, it can be with you in a flash.' Ruby heard her stifle a sob. 'Come home, sweetheart. This is where you belong, not in some magic box with a madman. Me and your gran, we're always here for you.'

Ruby cried all the way back to the TARDIS. After that phone call, the box seemed so strange again. She thought about all her journeys with the Doctor. The TARDIS had taken her to a space station in the far future, then back to 1963, an alien world – and so many other places. But what if… what if this had happened to her somewhere else? She could have been stranded halfway across the universe – or in another time zone altogether! Worse, she might have had to live through the 1960s. If she had, she might now be older than her own mother, her birth mother too.

But then, she could also have waited and discovered the truth, about when she was born. She could have lived through to Christmas 2004 and visited the church on Ruby Road where she was abandoned. Then she could have caught up with herself last year – her younger self, this self – if she was still alive. She could have met young Ruby and warned her: about what happened to the Doctor on these cliffs. But would that have stopped her, really…?

Probably not.

Besides, she knew that you couldn't interfere in your own personal history. The Doctor had made that clear on their first adventure in the TARDIS together. So the only option would have been for Ruby to wait.

More than sixty-one years. Her life might have ended before she'd even started living.

Perhaps being stranded here, now, just a few months ahead of her own time, was a blessing in disguise? She was only a few hundred miles from London. It could have been much worse. But at least Ruby had a choice, unlike the TARDIS.

'I might as well go back home,' she said, looking up at the box's windows. 'I haven't known you for that long, maybe this is what you do?' Then Ruby paused, considering, resting a cheek against the door. 'But if you come back,' she paused, 'I would love to see you again. I'd absolutely love it!'

She took a deep breath and stepped back. *Is this how it ends, then?*

Yes, she decided.

'Bye bye.'

As she turned to leave the TARDIS once and for all, she saw the Woman back beneath the tree: the same place she'd first spotted her.

'I'm going now,' Ruby called over. 'You win. Okay? You win! If you'd just stop talking and listen …' One final yell: 'You! Win!'

Satisfied, Ruby Sunday walked away. There was a train station not far from Glyngatwyg. A couple of branch lines would get her to Swansea, then it was straight through to London Paddington. She could put all this behind her. Wales, the Woman... maybe even the Doctor as well?

Safely on board the train to London, Ruby found herself drifting off. She was finally on her way home, back to Carla and Cherry, with Abdul and Mrs Flood (her bickering neighbours). She smiled as she watched the world whizz by and, as an inspector checked her ticket, life suddenly seemed so normal.

She thought about her time with the Doctor, the things they'd seen and secrets they'd shared. She'd witnessed the smog of '63 from a London rooftop... looked upon a future civilisation from a station in orbit... and now? Now, she was enjoying the familiar sight of inner-city houses sliding speedily past her window. Rooftop after rooftop, street after street, car after car and—

No, Ruby thought, *it can't be.*

She straightened in her seat, face pressed against the glass as her heartbeat started to quicken. Outside the carriage window, there was the Woman again.

Same woman, same clothing, same gestures. And always that very same distance.

She would vanish almost as quickly as Ruby glimpsed her, hidden behind a row of trees, or buildings, or tunnels. But Ruby knew she was there now. It didn't matter if they were passing fields or industrial wasteland, council estates or rural idylls – there she was. That Woman. She wasn't tied to the clifftops, or the circle, or Wales, or even the TARDIS. Whatever this was, whatever had happened, it wasn't over.

The Woman from Wales was coming with Ruby. Back to London.

She was coming home.

Chapter 6
Carla

When Carla Sunday heard the key in the door to the flat, she bounded from the bedroom, down the hall, carrying a basket filled with washing.

'Here she is, here she is, here she is, here she is!' Carla announced, pulling Ruby in for the biggest hug and kiss as she stepped through the door. 'All safe and sound!'

Ruby disguised her relief at being home by hugging her mother even tighter. For the last few days, the thought of being back home had seemed almost impossible, and now the familiar sight of her mum filled her with joy. Carla was wearing her favourite mustard cardigan (the one that her own mum, Cherry, had got her for Christmas) and the headscarf that Ruby had picked up in that boutique on Westbourne Grove.

'She's back!' Carla yelled down the hallway.

As they both pulled away from the hug, Ruby heard her grandmother Cherry calling back from her bedroom.

'I told her that man was no good! With his box of magic tricks! Some kind of guzum!'

Ruby popped her head round Cherry's door to say hello while Carla powered through to the kitchen. Like Carla's clothes, the room beamed brightly with colour – in this case, the fiercest yellow – and seemed almost designed to allow for the Sundays' excited bustling. Carla rinsed a few cups and flicked on the kettle, not missing a beat as Ruby returned.

'Maybe the Doctor went inside his box and … that's what men do,' Carla shrugged. 'They go into their sheds. And they potter. They have train sets and hobbies and things women should never know about.' She popped a teabag into each mug. 'I mean, I don't know, I've never had a garden, I've never had a shed, I've never had a man, but that's what they say. And your intergalactic nutcase. He's doing it on a cosmic scale. But he's still, essentially, inside his shed. Pottering. He must be!'

Ruby crossed to the kitchen window, staring down at the street below. As the kettle clicked off, Carla looked at her.

'I didn't tell you everything,' Ruby admitted, and Carla moved to join her at the window. She followed her daughter's gaze along the street, down to where the all-too familiar figure stood idly in the middle of the road.

'There's this woman,' Ruby explained to an oblivious Carla. Then, deciding it was easier to show than to tell, she took her mother's hand and led her outside.

As they stepped out onto the street, Ruby felt a blast of icy air. A strong November sun shone down from a clear blue sky, and yet it was cold now, colder than earlier. It reminded her instantly of those clifftops near Glyngatwyg, and her terrible hike through the snow – and there was the very same Woman, further away from the flat now they were outside, yet the very same distance from Ruby.

'You see?' Ruby asked her mother, moving forward, one step at a time. 'If I walk closer. I'm looking at her, d'you see? Keep watching her, can you see? Cos she's not moving, is she?'

'No,' confirmed Carla quietly, shaking her head.

Ruby stopped in her tracks to prove a point. 'And then I stop,' she paused, 'and she's moved.'

'Has she?' boggled Carla.

'How can you not tell?' Because however far Ruby had walked, the Woman had also travelled – somehow without either of them noticing. 'It's like she... affects people's eyes or something,' Ruby suggested. 'I know we've only gone forward 20 feet, but trust me. If we walked ten miles, she would still be further back.'

'You mean she'd be ten miles away?'

'No, she'd be...' Ruby hesitated, gesturing back to the Woman. How best to explain this? 'She'd be *that much* away.'

Ruby could tell that Carla wanted nothing more than to make sense of this for her daughter.

But in the end, her mum had to admit: 'I don't understand.'

'Neither do I,' sighed Ruby.

But that didn't mean they'd stop trying.

Five minutes later, Ruby stood on the street by herself, sizing up the Woman from a distance.

She found herself marching forward, eyes wide open, desperate to catch her stalker out – like some bizarre staring contest. But then a gust of wind would make her blink, or she'd catch her footing; a neighbour might distract her; and then there was that car alarm a couple of streets away...

None of these were significant in themselves, but each was enough to break Ruby's concentration.

A moment was all it took – an intake of breath, the flick of an eye – and the Woman would have imperceptibly moved. Slowly backing away…

Who was following who now, Ruby wondered? And just as she prepared to move closer, she was once again distracted; this time, by her own mother charging out from the flat. She clutched an old mobile phone in her hand, holding it triumphantly aloft.

'This is what we'll do!' said Carla excitedly. 'If I can approach her, then I'll phone you. I'll walk up to her, like this…' Carla mimed a short walk, lifted her phone to her ear and Ruby felt her own phone start to buzz. With a roll of her eyes, she answered, and mother and daughter exchanged a quick set of hellos.

'Then I can talk to her,' Carla continued, indicating the Woman, 'and you can hear what she's got to say.'

'I know, but I told you. Everyone she speaks to runs away!'

'Yes, but *Welsh people*.' Carla gave Ruby a playful nudge as if that explained everything. 'Trust me, darling. It's a plan!'

Ruby couldn't disagree. She'd been alone since all this began. It hadn't really occurred to her to find out what the Woman was *saying*, so maybe her mum had a point. The way that Enid and Lowri spoke about Wales – the castles and the torture and the blood – it came to them both so easily. Perhaps they were just superstitious? People like that, they wanted to believe. It wouldn't take much, on a dark and stormy night, with a stranger from out of town and a mysterious woman, for their imaginations to run away with them.

She only wondered what had made Joshua run and never come back.

'Just be careful, okay?' urged Ruby. She kept the phone to her ear, watching as her mother strode down the road towards the Woman.

But she wasn't the only one watching.

'Having a nice time?' It was their neighbour, Mrs Flood, putting her bins out ahead of collection day.

Ruby knew she'd want to know what was going on. It was a neighbourhood joke that nothing ever got past Mrs Flood. For someone constantly hiding themselves away, she seemed to know *everything*.

'Yeah, I'm just speaking to…' But Ruby wasn't allowed to finished her sentence.

'You're standing in the street… on the phone… to your own mother?'

Ruby nodded. 'Yeah.'

Mrs Flood paused. She looked at Ruby, alone in the road, then over to her mother. Then she squinted, as if not quite managing to make out who Carla was walking towards.

'Nothing to do with me,' Mrs Flood declared eventually, and with a shrug, she snuck back to her basement.

Ruby raised her phone back up to her ear. 'Mum?' she asked. 'What does she look like?'

'She looks like what she looks like,' Carla told her, matter-of-factly.

'But what does that mean?' urged Ruby.

Carla's voice was somehow flatter now. 'She looks like what she is,' her mother repeated.

Ruby watched as Carla slowly approached the Woman, phone still held to her ear. Her eyes were fixed; she didn't look back to Ruby once. Instead, she simply maintained her position a few feet from the stranger, listening as the Woman gestured again.

'Mum, what's she saying?' Suddenly, the air in the street felt heavy and the only sound on the phone was static. 'I can't hear. Mum. What's she saying?'

If Carla had heard Ruby, she didn't reply. Instead, the crackle grew louder – like this was something no one was meant to hear – and a terrible dread gripped

Ruby. She could see her mother slowly staggering backwards, dropping the phone to her side.

Then slowly, Carla turned, away from the Woman and back towards Ruby. She looked at her daughter with an expression she'd never once had before. It was hard to make out from this distance, but was that a look of fear on Carla's face?

'No, Mum, don't listen to her!' Ruby was screaming out loud now. 'Whatever she's saying, don't listen, Mum. Don't listen to her!'

It was already too late.

Carla Sunday fled in that moment. She ran, as fast as she could, from Minto Road: from the Woman, from the flat, and from her own daughter.

Ruby gave chase, crying out, 'Mum, don't do this, Mum, don't do this to me!' She pounded down the road, only slowing towards the end where Carla had vanished.

'Mum?' she yelled out.

No reply.

'Mum?' Ruby spun round, searching.

Still no reply.

'Mum?!?'

Ruby turned on her heels, surveying the area. Carla couldn't have just *disappeared*. They'd done a fun run the previous year and Ruby had beaten her (not that it was a competition). But that meant she could still catch up with her. They could talk. Nothing could be *that bad*, surely?

As if to answer her unspoken question, Ruby turned to see the Woman on her right. She was standing further up the adjacent street, framed against the low autumn sun. She wrung her hands apologetically, like she knew what would happen next.

Ruby almost didn't register it at first. The engine was all but silent. Instead, it was the screech of its tyres that caught her attention: a black London cab, thundering up the road towards Ladbroke Grove. Instinctively, Ruby turned, stepping back from the kerbside. It never quite occurred to her what was happening, not to begin with. But then she saw the driver, speeding past her, a familiar figure in the back seat of the cab, and all time seemed to slow in that moment.

Carla's eyes met Ruby's as the car roared away from her. It may have only been the briefest of glimpses, but it was still more than Ruby could cope with. The look of utter contempt on Carla's face ... the hatred in her eyes ... the same eyes that had once looked down on her in her bed, and watched her Nativities, even cried through all of Ruby's favourite movies.

'Mum!' Ruby screamed, as the taxi began to accelerate, but Carla turned her head away, eyes firmly on the road and her escape. 'Mum, please!' Ruby picked up her pace to chase after them, dropping her phone. 'Mum!'

But it was no good. The afternoon roads were clear and the car was too fast. Ruby watched as the cab passed the Woman, up the hill and out of sight. Then she collapsed by the roadside, catching her breath and crying.

She couldn't believe what was happening.

'She run away?' snapped Cherry accusingly, sitting up straight in her bed. 'What did you say to her?'

'It wasn't me, it was the woman.' Ruby paced up and down the flat's hallway, clutching her mobile. She'd been trying to get through to her mother for hours, ever since whatever happened had happened.

For the hundredth time, it went through to voicemail.

'Mum, phone me back and talk to me, that's all.' Ruby tried to keep her tone as considered as possible. 'Just tell me what she said.' A crack of vulnerability entered her voice as she added, 'Please, phone me back.'

* * *

The next day, Ruby woke up early to visit the chemist. She had to collect a prescription for Cherry and, in Carla's absence, pick up a few other supplies. They were low on bread and teabags, and it couldn't hurt to grab a few bits for dinner – she was planning to cook one of Cherry's favourites. The atmosphere at home was tense. A nice dinner was the least she could do.

A few hours later, as she walked back from the bus stop, Ruby tried calling Carla yet again. As expected, it went straight through to voicemail.

'I don't care if you're on answerphone,' Ruby said, 'I will keep calling, one hundred times a day.' She grabbed the key to the main front door from her pocket, turning it in the lock as she fumbled with her bags full of shopping. 'And you've got to come home! Gran is calling you *everything*!'

She began the hike upstairs to Flat 11.

'And if you come home, I'll make that shepherd's pie, the one they did on *Saturday Kitchen*, with the cheese?' Ruby reached the top of the staircase. 'Then we can sit down and just pretend that ...'

Ruby paused, twisting the key in the lock to Flat 11.

'Hang on,' she said, ending the call. She tried the key again. Then she tried another, just in case – perhaps she'd got the wrong one – but none of them worked, not one. It was like the TARDIS on that clifftop all over again, only this time…

'Oh you did not!' They must have changed the locks while Ruby was out. But she'd not even been gone that long. How the hell had they managed this?

Ruby dropped her shopping to the floor and banged on the door. She knew Carla had to be in there.

'Mum! Let me in!' Ruby yelled. 'Mum! Are you in there?'

But Carla didn't respond.

'Gran? Can you hear me?' Still no reply, not from either of them. 'You can't change the locks on me! You can't do this! You can't!'

In a sudden fit of rage, Ruby started hammering at the door. It had all become too much. Losing the Doctor was one thing, but to lose her family now, her home? She couldn't comprehend what that might mean, or how it had happened, or what she could do to resolve it. All she had left was her frustration and she would exhaust even that if she had to. She kicked wildly at the door, screaming louder and louder, determined to make as much noise as humanly possible.

Eventually, exhausted, she slumped by the door.

* * *

If time had slowed down before, now it seemed to speed up. Afternoon came and went in the blink of an eye. And for all that time, Ruby sat propped up against the door of Flat 11, waiting for something – anything – to happen. She knew they couldn't stay in there for ever. They'd have to open the door and engage with her at some point.

After an hour, Ruby heard a noise from the other side. A sort of shuffling sound, followed by a letter-sized envelope under the door. At first, she hoped it might be a message. If Carla couldn't bring herself to speak with Ruby, perhaps she felt more comfortable writing a note? Though the envelope felt thick, thicker than a single leaf of paper. How much could she have written, Ruby wondered?

The answer came quickly as she tore the paper open, revealing a selection of photographs – some Polaroids, others printed – all depicting Ruby with Carla and Cherry. Tears stung Ruby's eyes as she worked her way through them. She recognised most from the front of the fridge, but some had been torn from their picture frames, including the one that Cherry kept by her bed.

Looking through the images – all those memories and smiles – Ruby couldn't believe that this was over. Family meant more to Carla than anything.

Whatever that Woman had told her, it couldn't spoil the lives they'd shared. She was Carla's little girl, she always had been.

Ruby felt her phone begin to ring. As she answered, all that separated the call's participants was the simple hardwood door of a Notting Hill flat.

'I won't ask you again, Ruby,' Carla begged, exhausted. 'Please stop calling. And *go away*.'

This was progress, Ruby thought, at least they were talking now. She could work out what was wrong and make amends. 'But I'm your daughter,' she said.

'Except you're not,' paused Carla. 'Are you?' The silence in the second after that question would crush Ruby Sunday for ever. 'Even your real mother didn't want you ...'

With that, there was nothing more to be said. Anything Ruby wanted to utter got caught in her throat. She didn't know why Carla would say this, *how* she could say this. But the fact that she had now meant that this was the end for them. A terrible, numbing end.

Ruby wasn't quite sure how much longer she sat there. Her phone ran out of battery without any fanfare. She knew she could reach out to Trudy or Bex, they'd help her out (if she could only get hold of them).

But there wasn't any rush. Not now.

Too tired even for tears, Ruby leaned her head against the door, looking up – and there, through the skylight above her, she thought she saw the briefest flutter of snowflakes. The one constant throughout her life, always appearing to offer her comfort…

Never to be seen again.

Chapter 7
Kate

Ruby took a seat at Table 7: it was her favourite spot, outside her second-favourite café on the high street. The greasy spoon round the corner served a much better brew, but it was a little too tucked away.

She liked to watch the world go by.

For years, when she was in town, Ruby would head here (sometimes with friends, sometimes with Carla) and they'd sit with a juice or a coffee, inventing stories for all the people bustling round them. Some looked so happy, others so sad, a great many more … indifferent. It brought them comfort, though, to know that they weren't alone. There was always so much more going on around them: worlds and hopes and lives they could only dream of. And yet, in that precise moment, as had been the case for over a year, Ruby's focus was locked upon a single, solitary figure …

Until a cheerful, confident voice reclaimed her attention.

'I take it that's the woman?' The stranger blocked Ruby's view – a woman, strong and blonde, perhaps in her fifties, dressed in an immaculate forest green coat. She gestured over her shoulder, back to the Woman. 'Behind me, is that right?' she checked again.

Ruby nodded a simple 'Yes'.

'Good,' replied the newcomer, taking a seat. 'I'm Kate Lethbridge-Stewart.' She shook Ruby's hand like a promise. 'And I think I can help ...'

Their meeting wasn't accidental.

Kate ran an organisation called UNIT – more formally, the Unified Intelligence Taskforce.

Originally a paramilitary organisation established to deal with new and unusual menaces to mankind, it had regularly worked with the Doctor (across various incarnations) and had previously been led by Kate's father, the late Sir Alistair Gordon Lethbridge-Stewart (better known to most as the Brigadier).

Now, decades after its foundation, Kate had become UNIT's commander-in-chief, shifting its emphasis towards science and learning. Since the early twenty-first century, alien incursions had become increasingly difficult to cover up. The Nestene transgression, Christmas invasions, the fall of Canary Wharf. Then the Saxon conspiracy, planets in the sky, all the strange events around Cardiff. The infamous Year of the Slow Invasion. All this world's dead coming back to life as metal men. The Zygon Alliance.

That was when Kate had decided they had to become more public-facing.

For years, UNIT had hidden itself away on country estates across the Home Counties. Now they had a base in the middle of London; out and proud and defending the Earth… even if half the planet didn't believe that those threats were real.

People had heard the stories – oh, so many stories – but they were always written off as madness. If aliens had existed, people would know by now. 'It's not like the old days, before phones had cameras and Wi-Fi. You can't get away with anything these days.' But Kate knew you could get away with just about anything by hiding it all in plain sight. As Kate had pointed out to His Majesty, if you need to justify the expense, you may as well have something significant to show for it. Hence the UNIT Tower: a symbol in the heart of the capital city, screaming out for people to come to them with 'new and unusual menaces'.

Once Ruby's life had settled into some kind of normality after Glyngatwyg and Carla, she'd decided to pay UNIT a visit. She wasn't sure what she might find in UNIT Tower (or 'the Big Penguin' as it was known among Londoners). When she walked in, it was just another glossy corporate foyer – lots of glass, a nice big reception desk, security gates, even a water cooler. A polite young man named Jordan covered reception. He took her name, social media profiles and the nature of her request. When Ruby mentioned the Doctor and the TARDIS, she was promptly asked to take a seat around the corner. 'Someone will be with you shortly,' Jordan smiled.

Three minutes later, that 'someone' arrived. On the opposite side of the foyer, a pair of lift doors neatly parted to reveal a cheerful older woman in a smart pinstripe suit and Doc Martens. She headed straight over to Ruby.

'Hiya,' said the newcomer, sitting down next to her. 'They said you had some info on the Professor?'

Ruby looked at her, confused. 'Professor?'

'Sorry, Doctor. Force of habit. I'm Ace, by the way.'

'You're *ace*?'

'In every sense. Real name's Dorothy – you can see why I prefer Ace – and you must be Ruby Sunday?'

'Yeah, that's me.'

Ace smiled, shaking Ruby by the hand. 'Nice to finally meet you, Ruby Sunday!'

Ruby had sat there, listening, as Ace told her about her own time spent with the Doctor. As a girl, Ace had grown up in Perivale, a small town not far from Ealing, until a Time Storm whisked her away to a planet called Iceworld. She'd been 16 years old, a pawn in a game played by gods. She could have been trapped there for ever if the Doctor hadn't rescued her. He took her to so many places, showed her the universe. She learned so much by his side. But then, all good things ...

Ace had ended up back on Earth – but that story could wait, it was all a bit complicated. Now she worked for UNIT, on and off, as a freelancer, when she wasn't busy running her charity. 'There's more than one way to save the world!' Ace beamed. 'But enough about me, what about you? How long have *you* known the Doctor?'

'Not that long at all really,' Ruby admitted. 'In fact, I barely know the guy!'

'*Guy?*' That word seemed to surprise Ace. 'What's he like?'

'I thought you travelled with him.'

'Oh, I did,' Ace smiled again. 'But a very, *very* long time ago. Still, if the Doctor's gone missing …'

Ruby interrupted. 'It's not just that. There's this Woman. She's been following me. For months, ever since we landed in Wales. And it's mad, it's like, she scares people. Literally. She's scared them out of my life. Even my own mum.'

Ace glanced round the foyer. 'Is she here with us now?'

Ruby shook her head. 'It's tough in built-up areas. There's never enough space. But it's like she's always a certain distance away from me – and I mean, the *same* distance. So who knows? She could be a few floors above us … or spooking commuters on the Tube.'

'A fare-dodging supernatural entity,' joked Ace. 'You were right to come visit us.'

Ruby couldn't help laughing at the absurdity of it all. Was this what her life had become now – talking about phantom stalkers, sneaking onto public transport?

It seemed Ace recognised the expression. 'The Doctor showed me so much,' she offered gently, giving Ruby's hand a comforting squeeze. 'We went to so many places, did so much. We saved entire worlds!' Then her voice dropped to barely a whisper. 'And a lot of good people died. It can be a lot to take in when you're young.'

Ruby didn't let go of Ace's hand. For the first time in months, she felt safe. Ace was right: life around the Doctor was hard to explain. It was thrilling and joyous and deadly and strange and, above everything else, it was ludicrous.

But this put everything into perspective.

The Doctor had travelled to see the universe, to understand it all, to *learn*. Ruby had had a taste of that – her mind had been offered a glimpse of the possibilities – and since coming back to London, she felt so powerless. But now, sitting opposite Ace, her confidence was already rebuilding. Life didn't end with the Doctor and, from what Ruby could see, it could be better.

'We can help,' Ace said eventually, releasing Ruby's hand. 'I'm taking this right to the top! And trust me. She's helped all of us ...'

The next day, Ruby received a call from an unknown number. It was Jordan again, this time confirming that their boss would like to meet Ruby at 1300 hours on the day of her choosing. Ruby could pick the location, so long as it was 'out in the open'... which was how Kate came to be sat here now, listening to Ruby relate the events of the past 12 months.

'That was over a year ago,' said Ruby, explaining what had happened with Carla. 'She's taken out an injunction against me. My own mother. I thought about going back to Manchester, but I don't want to leave. Just in case. I've got this rubbish job at Kleinermann's, to make ends meet.'

'I think we can help with that,' Kate smiled, taking a sip from her cup of coffee. 'We have a tradition of helping the Doctor's former companions, once they return to a normal life.'

Ruby considered that phrase: 'a normal life'.

'I was hardly with him, really.'

'But it felt like a lifetime,' countered Kate with a knowing smile.

'Yeah.' From the second they met, Ruby somehow knew she could trust this woman.

'We had you on file after that event at Christmas,' Kate continued, sitting back in her chair. Then, remembering how chaotic the Doctor's life could be, she added: 'With the Goblins.'

'Oh my god, someone I can talk to about Goblins!'

Ruby's enthusiasm was infectious, and Kate was suddenly enjoying explaining her job to someone other than unimpressed government ministers.

'That's what we do,' she explained. 'In the UNIT

Tower. We're the Unified Intelligence Taskforce, created to investigate the extraterrestrial. And more and more, the supernatural. Things seem to be turning that way, these days.'

'And you worked with the Doctor?'

Kate hesitated. 'With him. Despite him. *Against him*, sometimes. And I adore him.' She leaned forward across the table, as if worried the universe might one day give her secret away. 'I can only say that now he's not here.'

'I won't say a word,' promised Ruby.

Then the smile across Kate's face faltered. 'I wish you'd got in touch with us sooner,' she sighed. 'We thought the Doctor was ... silent.'

Silent, Ruby considered. That was a nice way of describing it. Was the Doctor dead or had he gone someplace else? And if he'd gone, was it just her that he'd abandoned ... or the entire human race?

'I keep wondering how the world survives without him.'

'Well, that's classified,' Kate replied instantly. 'I think I can say, skin of our teeth. Although, I think this timeline might be ... suspended along your event.'

Ruby wondered what that meant: 'along your event'. But then, she'd seen more than enough to speculate.

There had been those 'events' when she was a child. Metal monsters flooding the skies over Tameside. She remembered Carla taking them all down into the basement, protecting them as Daleks bombarded the planet. But if aliens were still out there, and the Doctor wasn't around to defend the planet, why weren't they all invading ...?

Unless, the Earth continued to turn but was cut off somehow? '*Suspended along your event*' – ever since the Doctor had vanished inside that circle ...

Yes.

That sort of made sense.

'And you can take us to the TARDIS?' prompted Kate.

Ruby nodded enthusiastically. 'Yeah, it's just sitting there, I'm surprised no one's reported it.'

'It has a perception filter. People notice it, but ... sort of don't.' Kate paused for a moment. Then she swivelled to face the Woman. 'I wonder if it's connected, if landing a perception filter on top of that circle has affected things?'

'Well, maybe,' Ruby considered. 'Cos she's got a perception thing too. Like, no one at work has complained about the old woman standing outside every day. It's like they see her, but they don't notice her.'

She racked her brain for examples. 'I once positioned her in front of a police car. They just drove around her!'

'And... if you sit in a room with no windows?'

'I can't see her. But I know she's there,' Ruby said with more urgency. '73 yards away. I've measured it, a hundred times. I have measured it *thousands* of times, it's 73 yards. I went and stood at the top of the Shard, and I knew she was 21 floors below. 21 floors is 73 yards.'

A chill breeze made her shiver. 'The funny thing is, I prefer to sit outdoors. I like to know I can see her.'

'But if you went on a plane..?'

'Or a boat, I know. But ...' Ruby started to hesitate. 'I don't. Because I keep thinking. If I cut her off, I might die. Or she might die. Does that sound mad?'

'It sounds wise,' Kate reassured her, giving Ruby the kind of look the Doctor would give her: a look that said she was ready for anything the universe had to throw at them. 'That's what we do, all of us,' Kate continued, 'we see something inexplicable and invent the rules to make it work. Mankind saw the sunrise and created God ... or we saw the arrival of a Sontaran, one or the other.'

Kate's tablet bleeped discreetly in her hand. She glanced at its screen.

'And I can confirm,' she smiled, studying the device's analytics, 'our scan says 73 yards exactly.' She looked up from the tablet, nodding across the street. 'I hope you don't mind, I didn't come alone.'

Ruby glanced over in that direction, following Kate's gaze. Maybe she'd been too wrapped up in the Woman to notice, but suddenly she was aware of an inconspicuous van parked outside the shops across the street. It sported what looked like a host of state-of-the-art scanning technology, running from roof to windscreen. Then further along the pavement, Ruby spotted three or four couples – some in plain clothes, others in sleek black uniforms – all monitoring the vicinity via mobile phones and earpieces. They moved in discreet loops to avoid detection, overlooked by an oblivious London public, too preoccupied to notice anything out of place.

Kate indicated the space behind Ruby, who turned to see a young, fit couple pacing outside a betting shop, clearly armed and there to protect her.

'Don't worry,' Kate urged, 'you're quite safe.'

'No, it's fine, it's great!' With relief, Ruby looked back at the Woman. Not too far behind her, Ruby noticed another similarly innocuous couple, armed and pacing, surveying their target.

Without looking back, Kate explained: 'We've photographed her. But this is the only image we can get.'

She pinched the edges of an image with her fingers, expanding it outwards, then handed the device to Ruby for her assessment. The screen depicted the scene at the end of the street: a high-resolution photo of the environment, signs and licence plates depicted in perfect clarity...

But the Woman herself was a blur. Little more than a clumsy smudge of bloated pixels.

'I know,' Ruby said. She'd been through all this before. 'I tried, I bought the most expensive camera, and... I still can't zoom in on her face.'

'Our equipment is a bit more sophisticated, and yet. She only registers from the point of view of an average person's twenty-twenty eyesight from 73 yards away...' Kate made the calculations. '219 feet...'

'66.7 metres,' said Ruby, simultaneously. She'd made those same calculations a very long time ago, wondering if the distance could be significant.

'Well, it proves you're not going mad,' Kate reassured her.

And on hearing those words, Ruby laughed with a relief she'd not felt in months. 'Thank you!' she cried, triumphant.

'So. There's only one more option.' Kate slipped the tablet back in her pocket. 'Let's bring her in.'

'But she won't!' protested Ruby, a little uncertain. 'If you talk to her, she … *does* something!'

'My staff have full psychic training,' Kate informed her, coolly. 'We have telepathic dampeners. Mesmeric shielding. And necklaces of silver and salt in case of witchcraft. Don't worry. You're with experts, now.'

There was no warmth in her reassurance. This Kate Lethbridge-Stewart meant business. Clearly she intended to take the Woman into custody and Ruby guessed that nothing would stop her.

As she turned to address her team, Ruby suddenly realised that Kate had been wearing an earpiece this whole time. She activated the comms and then, with gentle efficiency, issued the simplest of instructions: 'Go, go, go.'

From nowhere, Ruby heard a surge of noise. It came from all around them. Along the street, footsteps thundered towards the Woman as each and every operative hurried towards her. Seventy-three yards from the café, a pair of armoured UNIT trucks screeched onto the pavement and slammed on their brakes, allowing a throng of armed UNIT soldiers to burst through their doors. Experts disembarked while ground support escorted frightened onlookers away from the Woman.

Ruby looked up as a helicopter roared overhead, drawing her attention to the rooftops. Above each and every shop, she could now see snipers, creeping forward with their weapons and taking aim: every available member of UNIT was on high alert. She watched as Kate's calm and pleasant demeanour slipped and a ruthless efficiency took hold.

'Do not talk to her,' Kate instructed her people, 'do not look her in the eyes, do not engage with her in any way, just bring her in.'

Ruby shifted to watch the Woman, but then the air grew heavy and cold. Already she knew what would happen, as the soldiers drew closer and closer. Were they talking to her? Was she talking to them? She could just about make out that all-familiar shrug, always directed at Ruby.

The soldiers followed the Woman's glare, all the way back up to Ruby, whose eyes were now filling with tears. She could feel their stare burn through her.

'I said, do not engage,' Kate repeated more fiercely.

Suddenly Ruby heard something unusual come through her earpiece. Was it feedback, some kind of message? She wanted to ask what it was Kate could hear but knew it was pointless. 'No. Don't,' she warned. 'Don't listen to her, Kate. Don't!'

The air grew heavy around them as Kate turned to face her. She peered at Ruby with such a cold and terrible look – contempt and disdain.

Ruby could only gaze back as the commander stared her down.

Then, Kate issued her final order with just one word: 'Disengage.'

As swiftly as they'd arrived, UNIT vanished from sight. Snipers disappeared from their positions on the rooftops; soldiers on the ground slammed into trucks which scorched away. Even Kate marched briskly into a car, escorted by two of her bodyguards, both of whom glanced back at Ruby to ensure Kate's safe distance. Within seconds, the doors to her car slammed shut and Kate was away, without so much as a glance back at Ruby.

Ruby looked all around her, hope and relief draining away. Only seconds ago, there had been so many people. Now there was no Kate, no soldiers, no protection. Just Ruby and the Woman.

Was this what the Woman wanted – to isolate her?

'All right,' screamed Ruby, losing her patience. 'All right, all right!'

She threw her arms out angrily, smashing her coffee cup.

A waitress came running over. 'Oi!' she yelped. 'D'you mind?'

'Yes,' cried Ruby again, ignoring her, 'I said, all right!'

Ruby never spoke to UNIT again. She often got the sense that someone was watching her from afar, someone other than the mysterious Woman, but whoever they were would have been trained to go unnoticed. In a strange way, Ruby was grateful for the attention because, although the Woman never attempted to harm her, her continued presence always felt like a kind of threat. Whatever had scared UNIT off, it had to be significant – in which case, there was no way they wouldn't be monitoring the situation.

For a good few years, Ruby really believed they might be able to change things.

But nothing changed.

Chapter 8
Ruby

In the years that followed, Ruby tried her best to live a normal, simple life.

The Woman wasn't leaving; she'd come to accept that. So instead she found another way to exist. Where before she'd always kept the Woman in sight, now Ruby became less guarded. Sometimes, she'd choose a discreet little coffee shop hidden away in a labyrinth of alleyways, knowing the Woman would be safely out of sight. Then she could meet with friends, Ruby decided; she could hang out with colleagues from work – but she still couldn't risk them properly noticing the Woman who followed her. Whatever it was she said, it seemed to terrify people. Her own mother had …

No. Best not to think about that.

After a couple of months, Ruby chose to start seeing a therapist, to open up about her sense of isolation.

She knew it wasn't all in her mind, she understood the cause, but perhaps there was a way of coping with this: the lack of control, the isolation. Maybe Ruby had the power to change things.

For several sessions, Ruby explained what she'd been experiencing to a nice young man named Dominic. He tried to help her guide her thoughts, make her consider what this 'Woman' represented. Was it something to do with her past? Was it an embodiment of her feelings surrounding her mother – her birth mother, he meant, not Carla; they'd cover that in a different session altogether. And Ruby told him what he wanted to hear. She speculated about why the Woman might appear the way she did, always at a distance, driving people away – of course it was to do with her mother – and for a while, Ruby almost believed it …

Until the day came that Dominic encountered the Woman outside his office. Perhaps he'd engaged so much with Ruby's story that he couldn't avoid the connection? And this Woman looked exactly as Ruby had stated, to the point Dominic thought it might be a joke. But then, as he got closer, he learned the truth. The Woman must've told him all that she'd said to everyone else; everyone but Ruby, who could never get close enough.

Dominic cancelled all his sessions for the rest of the day and instructed Ruby to never make contact again. He even told her not to recommend him to anyone else, so afraid was he of hearing her name again, even in passing.

These incidents became more frequent. For Trudy's birthday, they attended a concert at the O2 Arena where, for the shortest of times, Ruby almost allowed herself to forget about the Woman entirely. Then after the warm-up act, she looked down and saw that familiar shock of white hair standing sentinel in the aisle next to their seating block. She stood with her back to them, facing the stage, several rows and 73 yards away, almost as if she had come there to take in the show.

Most people absentmindedly made their way past this strange old woman, squeezing by to take their seats. But one of the stadium stewards engaged her directly – the Woman was blocking an aisle, which Ruby supposed must be against their emergency code. Whatever he said to the Woman, the response she gave looked to have chilled the blood in his veins. The steward glanced up to where Ruby was sitting and, without saying a word, he ran, scrambling up the stairwell to the fire exit.

Some attendees nearby laughed as he lost his footing, landing with a thump on the steps, but only Ruby understood what he was doing.

The Woman remained for the rest of the evening, alone in the aisle. Ruby wondered if she enjoyed what she was seeing, longing to see her cheer and break into applause ...

Instead, the Woman's bearing never altered. She simply shrugged through hit after hit.

No pleasing some people, thought Ruby.

Ruby's everyday life became more and more routine. She kept herself to herself at work, grabbed a sandwich each day from the café and ate in the staffroom. She tried her best to fly under the radar.

When bosses asked about aspirations, Ruby always maintained she was happy where she was. The more she could do to avoid meetings, or members of the public, the better. She was even happy with night shifts and working from home.

Her home life became more stable, albeit through more than unpleasant circumstances.

Two years after she left the Sundays' flat, she learned that her gran had passed away in her sleep. Carla had not contacted her, but now solicitors were getting involved. It turned out that, for all of Carla's nagging, Cherry had never got round to updating her will and Ruby had been named as a beneficiary (a not insubstantial amount, enough to provide a deposit on a flat and a little security).

Carla tried her best to contest it, of course, but the law was the law. The solicitors tracked down Ruby, breaking the news, and talked her through the relevant processes. Carla had made it clear, to absolutely anyone and everyone who might listen, that she wanted nothing to do with Ruby. If this was the price she had to pay to get her out of her life for good, then so be it. In her eyes, this was a final gift from her mother.

This reaction upset Ruby more than anything else. She'd come to terms with what had happened that day but had somehow always imagined – always *hoped* – that they might one day be reconciled. Now Cherry was no longer with them, that wasn't possible, and it seemed only to have made Carla more determined to hold her silence.

Ruby respected their wishes.

She'd had to avoid the funeral, but made sure to visit the grave at the first opportunity. She went at night to avoid being seen, laying down a simple bouquet of flowers on the grave.

The headstone made no mention of her – only the 'BELOVED MOTHER OF CARLA SUNDAY' – but then Ruby had never expected it to. She thought about writing a note but reconsidered; she didn't want to be the cause of any more upset. Besides, she didn't have to write down the words to know how she was feeling. She didn't even have to say them out loud. She just needed to be there, to say goodbye.

'Thank you, Gran,' she whispered, shedding a tear. 'Night night.'

Ruby stayed there for over an hour, on a bench beneath a tree with a perfect view. The cemetery was vast, with so many gravestones: hundreds of lives that had been and gone and eventually been forgotten.

Ruby knew the Woman was with her but never once saw her, not that she was looking. It made for a welcome change, though. It was almost as if the Woman knew Ruby needed this moment. The time and space to grieve.

In 2029, Carla sold the flat in Notting Hill and moved back to Manchester. She didn't leave a forwarding address.

Ruby, meanwhile, found a small apartment on the Powell Estate in Southwark. She didn't have much to take with her, just a few suitcases of clothes, a shoebox of memories ... and the Woman she took with her everywhere.

She didn't have a lot of money but enough to get by. The first Christmas living alone was somehow the hardest. In previous years, she'd always spent it with family or friends. Now, she was all alone on Christmas Eve. It was her twenty-fifth birthday.

A few people still kept in touch and sent her greetings cards – a messy combination of Christmas and birthday, rolled into one. Some of them even made a point of remembering how old she actually was, which made Ruby feel a bit less forgotten. It was a difficult time of year, she always told herself. People have lives of their own, especially now. Her friends were all getting older, settling down. Perhaps Ruby should too? Was this her, settling down, she wondered?

She poured herself a modest glass of wine, then crossed to her equally modest Christmas tree and looked out through the window. It wasn't quite Tameside, she thought, but it was home. For the moment, anyway.

Below her, she saw the Woman alone in the courtyard, standing patiently in the rain, and Ruby raised her glass in a silent toast to her eternal companion, the burden she bore.

Life is what you make it, she kept telling herself. And she was now more determined than ever to make something of it.

She tried to date in the hope of meeting someone significant, not that she came into contact with many new people these days. But, every now and again, she'd take the risk and put herself out there.

That was how she'd met Frank Hinchey. He was a year older than her, friend of a friend – good job, lovely teeth, pleasant demeanour – in short, perfect boyfriend material. They had similar hobbies and interests, and he could make her laugh like a drain. He was a great cook and expert listener; they'd enjoy evenings on the sofa round his, or nights at the theatre or open-air concerts.

They were good. For a time.

One day, after months of going out, Frank was struck by the fact he'd never set foot in Ruby's flat.

Was she embarrassed by him? Or worse, hiding something *from* him? Another man, perhaps? No, that wasn't her style. But then, how well did he know her, really? She was so cagey about her past, and always distracted, like she was looking over his shoulder for someone better.

In the end, Frank decided to have it out with her. He'd try to make it a conversation rather than a confrontation. He planned an evening where he'd cook them both dinner then ask her the question. As it turned out, he just couldn't wait.

It was a Saturday afternoon when he prompted 'the conversation'. The sun was shining, and Ruby had agreed to go with him for a stroll round the local park. After an hour, they came back to the fountain, where they'd met on their very first date, and Frank bought them both a takeaway latte from a parked-up coffee van.

It was now or never, he thought. Dinner could wait; he had to know.

Together, they sat on a bench, watching as the world passed them by: a blur of joggers and dog walkers, mothers and businessmen. No one stood out particularly... except for the Woman, who stood on a slope, watching from afar. But Frank's attention was only on Ruby, even if hers was no longer on him.

'... and y'know, I'm not complaining,' Frank continued. 'But I say, let's go away, let's go to New York. And you say no. So, I keep thinking – I don't want you to take this the wrong way, but I've got to ask – is there someone else?'

Ruby looked at him. She seemed weary and defeated.

'Yes,' she said.

Her life began to fall into a pattern. Every December, she dusted the tree from the top of her closet and started to get in the festive spirit. Cards would arrive – some for Christmas, some for her birthday – but notably fewer and fewer, year on year. And whenever she met someone new, however good and attractive they were, her attention would always wander back to the Woman.

Nothing happened without a reason, Ruby believed that firmly.

So why was *this* still happening?

Why was the Woman still with her?

Ruby got on with living her life as best she could.

The problem was, that kind of life wasn't best for everyone.

Now she was sat in a London arcade, 34 years old, opposite her latest boyfriend, Sanjay Miah. He was always so neatly turned out – nice jacket, checked shirt, no creases – and he'd do absolutely anything to make Ruby happy. But even he was beginning to struggle.

'It's just sometimes,' he began, apologetically, 'I get the impression you're not really listening. Like you're drifting off and thinking of something else.' He waited for a response but Ruby said nothing. She'd done it again. 'Well, like now, to be honest!'

Ruby nodded as Sanjay fell silent – couldn't agree more, that's what they wanted to hear – while all the time, she kept glancing to the Woman in the entrance, blocking her exit.

Would there ever be a way out of this?

By the time Ruby turned 40, she'd grown accustomed to solitude. Now Christmas became routine. A token handful of cards sat shyly by the window, and her tree was dressed more with dust than decorations. But none of that mattered. Christmas Eve was *her* time, always had been.

That night, she crossed to the window and raised a mug of tea in silent acknowledgement, as was tradition. The world around them may be changing – new streetlights and cars and office blocks – but she could always rely on her constant companion.

However much the Powell Estate may have altered, the Woman would always be there for her, standing 73 yards away, rain or shine.

* * *

After suffering recurring headaches, Ruby was referred to an optician and told she was long-sighted. She needed glasses. Now she took a peculiar comfort in removing them. The resulting smear swallowed her vision almost immediately, meaning that sometimes, just occasionally, she could pretend that the Woman was no longer there.

Alone, yet never alone...

Eighteen months later, it was 2046. Ruby had been dating Rufus Bray for almost a year. Of everyone she'd met, he'd undoubtedly been the most patient. She'd felt able to open up to him – not about the Woman, of course, but about her family; everything that had happened with Carla and Cherry; the way her birth mum had left her outside the church on Ruby Road.

Tonight though, Ruby Sunday was decidedly uncomfortable. She'd made the mistake of letting Rufus choose the venue: an admittedly nice gastropub not far from Oxford Street. The issue was that they were indoors, and the windows were shuttered, so Ruby had no idea of the Woman's location. They'd now been trapped together for so many years that Ruby found her presence reassuring; whereas now the Woman was lost to her, somewhere 73 yards away, out of sight.

She could be interacting with *anyone* – and that unsettled Ruby more than anything.

She made repeated excuses to visit the bathroom and kept straining on her chair for a better view, but nothing was helping. Worse, Rufus was feeling ignored – sweet, patient Rufus, he'd always had so much time for her. That's why Ruby had shared so much with him.

'Thing is,' Rufus began, 'I know you've had a tough time. That whole thing with your mother is weird, okay. But it's hard for me, sometimes, y'know. And sometimes, I think…'

Ruby nodded as she glanced from side to side, hoping for some hint of the Woman somewhere. But then something else grabbed her attention: a screen, projected onto the window of one of the dining booths. Some kind of party political broadcast, nothing remarkable. And yet Ruby felt drawn to it.

There was a man – clean-cut, mid-thirties, with raven hair and emerald eyes – standing behind a podium in some kind of studio. There were other participants too, but he seemed to shine. A political golden boy.

As he spoke, she saw his name emblazoned in the chyron:

ROGER AP GWILLIAM.

'The most dangerous Prime Minister in history...' Suddenly, the Doctor's words echoed in her head, encouraging Ruby. He'd uttered them over two decades ago, but in that moment, it felt like he was right there next to her. She'd forgotten what it had felt like, to be with the Doctor, and now she knew for certain that this was important. Nothing else mattered.

She leaned forward on her stool, listening intently to the broadcast.

'What's your take on this, Roger ap Gwilliam?' asked an unseen presenter. The young man seemed to glitter with pride, all smiles.

'No public school for me!' Gwilliam said from his podium. 'I've done hard work, I started out as a pizza delivery boy, I worked on a fruit stall in Swansea Market. The Steel Mills. Hospital porter. Security guard. I was a jack of all trades!' He smiled a wolfish grin. *'Mad Jack*, they'd call me!'

Ruby felt a shiver run down her spine as she remembered that night in Glyngatwyg: the pub, Y Pren Marw; Lowri and Enid, Lucy and Ifor; the story they'd shared – Mad Jack. And that scroll, the one they said she shouldn't have read. The strands of that circle were tugging at her now, looping back to form connections.

It might mean nothing, sure. But Ruby had learned a very long time ago, on a Goblin ship in the sky with her very best friend: never ignore a coincidence.

'…you're so remote,' Rufus continued, blathering earnestly. 'It's like you're not quite there. Even in bed. It's like you're always a distance away.'

For the first time that night, Ruby laughed, suddenly focusing entirely on her date.

'*Semperdistans* is the word,' she said. Then she hopped from her stool, still smiling, picked up her coat and stepped over to where Rufus was sitting.

'Look,' she explained, 'you were sweet, and this was nice, but you're right. It was never going to work. And that's my fault – except for the bed thing.' She patted his hand. 'Because that was really, really you. But it's taken me all this time to realise what I'm here to do.'

'Which is what …?' Rufus asked.

Ruby grabbed her bag and beamed. 'I'm going to save the world.' Then with a quick kiss on the cheek, she was gone.

And Rufus had got his answer.

As Ruby left the venue, she looked both ways, as if crossing the street. To her left, past a row of shops, the Woman was waiting.

She'd been waiting so long.

But this was their time now, Ruby knew it.

'Come on!' Ruby called, striding off with her head held high. 'We've got work to do.'

Chapter 9
Roger

Roger ap Gwilliam's face stared down at Ruby, from all the way across the street. His carefully posed publicity portraits were emblazoned in red, white and blue behind the windows of a disused shopping unit, now converted into the Albion Party's official Campaign Headquarters. Each poster promised a *Bigger, Better, Bolder Britain*.

Dressed to impress and ready for whatever the political landscape might throw at her, Ruby marched through Kennington, crossed the high street and burst through the doors of Albion HQ. Even then, she didn't stop moving. The staff were all busy at desks, or criss-crossing the room to answer phones and hand out flyers. Banners and balloons were adorned with Roger's well-rehearsed smile.

It never quite reached the eyes though, Ruby noticed.

Following the flow of the office, she came to a desk manned by 'Craig Deloach: Team Leader' (as designated by his official Albion name tag, also in red, white and blue). He smiled with an infectious, efficient energy, and wore an expression that instantly seemed to ask people: *How can I help you?*

'Hi there,' Ruby blustered, offering a smile as infectious as his was. 'I just wanted to offer my services! I thought I'd volunteer.'

'Okay, good news,' replied Craig, always happy to welcome new recruits. 'What for, exactly?'

'Oh, anything. Anything at all! I just think Roger ap Gwilliam is amazing. And I want to help the cause!' Ruby watched as Craig's enthusiastic grin grew even wider. 'I've got a thousand pounds in savings,' she continued. 'I can donate that, right now. I'll do leaflets, or answering the phones, just tell me what to do, I'll do anything! Hey,' she joked, 'I'll even carry the coats!'

Ruby laughed and Craig laughed with her.

Six weeks later, Ruby was carrying the coats for Albion's media team. She and a group of Roger's aides (all male, not that she'd remark upon that again) stood on the sidelines of Golden Boy's latest interview, deep within the bowels of Broadcast Centre.

Nobody knew whether any broadcaster was truly impartial any more. Everyone – left, right or centre – claimed to have evidence to the contrary. But whether or not such an agenda existed, everyone knew that this particular interview wouldn't be easy. Sir Amol Rajan had been a reporter for forty years and had a well-earned reputation for not letting his interviewees off the hook.

Roger's campaign, in turn, had not been without its problems. His choice of rhetoric, in particular, had stoked concern from opponents, with questions in both Houses of Parliament and a host of failed petitions across social media.

If anyone was in a position to undermine Roger ap Gwilliam, it was Sir Amol. Both men now confronted one another across the ten-foot faux glass desk of the *Hotline* TV studio. It was one of the last physical sets remaining in broadcasting, a deliberate nod to solicit more trust from viewers. After the Deep Fake scandals of 2037, all journalism was heavily scrutinised for any party political content by adjudicators from the Broadcast Standards Committee.

Ruby watched Roger and Sir Amol full-frame on the studio monitors, aware that 73 yards through the wall, the Woman was out there.

Gwilliam, meanwhile, was in the middle of defending his controversial manifesto. 'If there's a crime, if there's a danger, if there's a virus, we will have our people mapped,' he insisted vehemently. 'We'll know where you're from, and who you are. And if you want that kept secret ... then I'd like to know, what are you hiding?'

Sir Amol broke in: 'But the government says—'

'What government?' Gwilliam sneered. 'The government has collapsed. In shame. In absolute shame, Amol. So now's the time. To vote. So Britain can find its voice! And its pride. And its future.'

'But the point is,' Sir Amol continued, determined not to let his subject off the hook, 'if the people are worried about anything, it's the cost of living. And inflation. And a price cap set at £15,000. But you want to spend billions – you have pledged to spend £65 billion – on *nuclear weapons.*'

The already noiseless studio fell even more silent. A dread hush descended over the media team, punctured only by Gwilliam's own brand of effortless charm as he considered the question.

'Amol,' beamed Gwilliam breezily. 'I'm a Welshman. I'm from Wales. That's what the "ap" in my name means, it's not like those apps we had on our phones in the

old days, it's Welsh for "son of". I am a *son of* Wales.'
Suddenly, his tone became more confrontational. 'And
the Welsh know what it's like to be oppressed. It has
taught me to say: no more.' Roger looked straight
into camera. 'That is what I'm saying: no more. I want
Great Britain to say: no more. So yes! I have pledged
to defend our borders and set us up on high, as the
greatest nation in the world.'

Off camera, his team automatically nodded.

'But we're members of NATO,' protested Sir Amol.

'And when did NATO ever fire a nuclear missile?
Ever?' Roger leaned back in his chair now, citing
examples. '2031, the Great Russian War, nothing!
Not a single rocket. That's not a deterrent. That's a
scrap heap.'

'I'm sorry. Excuse me. But…' Amol's appalled
expression said it all. 'Are you saying, you *want* to fire
a nuclear missile?'

Ruby studied Roger closely on the monitor. For a
moment, she thought it was a technical fault, as his
entire expression seemed to freeze: that same, self-
satisfied grin dominated his face and didn't change.
But then it faltered, briefly.

Roger had no answer for this.

There *was* no reasonable answer he could give.

His voice dropped along with his smile as he leaned across to an aide off-camera. 'We'll cut that bit out, yeah?' he whispered. When his assistant duly nodded, Roger's smile returned and he sat back upright, confronting Sir Amol as if nothing had happened. A dangerous glint in his eye.

Time to move on now, he dared. *Next question.*

Before Sir Amol could react, a floor manager sprang into view, as if from nowhere.

'Okay, ladies and gents, let's take ten there please!'

Seven minutes later, Sir Amol's flagship interview with Roger ap Gwilliam was concluded. As the production team bustled and cameras reset for the following feature, Roger and his Yes Men were engaging in small talk, making plans. The interview had been a success – or at least, it would be by the time it was broadcast.

'Very good, Steve,' said Roger, taking his associate by the hand and shaking it firmly. He then leaned into his ear and added, 'Have a word, I don't think we need Sir Amol, do we? Sort that out.' Satisfied that Sir Amol's indiscretion would be edited out of existence, Roger patted Steve on the shoulder and moved down the line. 'Danny, talk to comms about next week. Immediately.' And, like Steve before him, Danny nodded.

'Craig,' Roger sniffed, 'get the car.'

'Yes, sir,' Craig responded instinctively. He was the only one out of all of them to speak. In their collective hurry, each man crossed to Ruby and snatched up their coat. There were no other words, no thank yous; in that respect, they followed their master's lead. Then they fled from the studio floor in a scramble of diligence, leaving Roger ap Gwilliam alone with Ruby Sunday.

He politely removed his coat from her grasp and appraised her coolly. She was older than he might have expected. Typically, he liked his team young. He said they promoted the right kind of energy. They were the faces of Britain's future after all – or at least, that's what Roger liked them to believe. His would be the only face that mattered, the only one that people would ever remember.

He'd make certain of it.

Ruby held Roger's gaze. She was a little unnerved that, after all these weeks, he'd finally decided to notice her.

'Are you with us?' he asked with an empty smile.

'Yes,' she said. 'My name's Ruby.'

Twenty years ago, she'd have commanded his attention without even trying. Now, in the dim purple light of the studio, she had to consider every word.

'Tell me,' murmured Roger, sidling closer; Ruby noticed him flick the switch of his radio mic so no one could be listening. 'What about *her*?' he asked, gesturing over to a group across the studio. 'That girl over there. Is she one of ours?'

Ruby knew immediately who he was talking about – Roger always seemed to ask about the shy ones – and she felt a shiver run down her spine as she answered.

'She's with Danny's team,' Ruby told him. 'She's a volunteer.'

'What's her name?'

'Marti Bridges.'

'Marti,' Roger repeated, his lips wet with glee. 'Boy's name.' Then he smiled – no, more than smiled, he grinned – and Ruby felt her blood run cold.

She watched as Roger shucked on his coat and sauntered over to Marti. The shy young girl, dressed in a blue sweater and paisley skirt, looked up in awe and shook his hand.

With effortless charm, Roger took Marti's hand in his, shook it firmly, and although Ruby couldn't make out what he was saying, she knew in the pit of her stomach that it couldn't be good.

Finally, Roger's smile reached his eyes, as he escorted Marti away.

Chapter 10
Marti

'We need saturation!' Craig commanded, throwing open the door to his Albion-branded van to reveal box upon box of leaflets. 'Every house! Don't skip a single front door.' He handed a box to Ruby. 'Doesn't matter if they like him, doesn't matter if they don't. We just need the name Roger ap Gwilliam *everywhere*.' As more volunteers came forward, more boxes left the van. 'Get to it!'

The Albion team dispersed, and Ruby set off along her designated route, tackling house after house on street after street, posting a glossy leaflet through each of their letterboxes. One side declared the desire for a *Bigger, Better, Bolder Britain*, while the reverse featured an overly airbrushed photo of Roger himself.

Ruby enjoyed folding each leaflet in half to escape his gaze.

'I'm not voting for him!' one man told her, snatching the leaflet from Ruby's hand before she even reached his door. He made a show of ripping it to pieces in front of her. 'He's the most appalling man I've ever seen!'

'Oh, I know!' agreed Ruby. 'He's unstoppable!' Then she continued down the street, distributing leaflet after leaflet, all under the Woman's watchful gaze.

When Election Night came, there was no doubt at Albion Headquarters that Ruby had been instrumental in getting the message out there and doing her bit for the cause. Her enthusiasm had been singled out as an example to her fellow volunteers. If politics was about the people, Ruby Sunday was the sort of person Albion needed ... though that didn't stop Craig from taking her aside for a quiet word.

'Look, Ruby, you've been great,' he said. 'And you know they've got big jobs going, in party headquarters, but ...' He took a long deliberate breath. 'This is Roger. He's not really going to promote *women*. Is he?'

This was the first sincere thing she'd heard Craig say.

'And that's absolutely fine,' replied Ruby. 'I'm not here for a promotion. I'm here to change the world.'

* * *

Hours later, shortly before three o'clock in the morning, Roger ap Gwilliam was declared winner of his Kennington constituency. An overwhelming majority had already been predicted, and now Roger was broadcasting live on every channel, speaking as the nation's new Prime Minister.

As his rival candidates looked on, Roger took to the podium, thanked the returning officer and bathed in a sea of fervent cheers. Indulgently, he purred into the microphone, hitting every word with more and more force.

'I will go!' he grinned. 'To His Majesty!' The crowd whooped. 'And prepare!' He paused again, enjoying the moment. 'For government!'

And with that, the crowd went wild.

Back at Albion Headquarters, Roger's team cheered even harder. Most of them had spent the day at polling booths, handing out flyers and chatting with voters. Others had come straight from day jobs, but still found time to change into their Albion-branded uniforms. This was a day that they would never forget: the culmination of all their hard work. Most hadn't realised, of course, that by morning 90 per cent of them would be surplus to requirements.

Dressed in an Albion T-shirt of her own, Ruby looked round the office, horrified. She'd been so convinced that this was what she was meant to do. But now she was here, in this room, at that precise moment – surrounded by so many people who truly *believed* – it all felt so wrong.

The Doctor's words repeated in her head: *the most dangerous Prime Minister in history*... and she'd been part of the team to make it happen. Holding the coats, generating revenue, chatting to people door-to-door. This couldn't all be for nothing.

She crossed over to one of the windows, peering through a gap in the branded posters. Outside, 73 yards away, the Woman stood reassuringly under a street lamp. Nothing had changed, then. Still there was work to be done.

Craig knocked back a drink and struck up a chant. '*Ro-ger, Ro-ger, Ro-ger!*'

More and more of the team joined in. '*Ro-ger! Ro-ger! Ro-ger!*'

Away from all the cheers and celebration, Marti Bridges sat alone in a quiet corner. Ruby caught her eye across the room and was coming towards her.

This made Marti's heart begin to race.

She liked Ruby, more than the rest of them; Ruby had an honest face. But that made Marti anxious. Sometimes she worried about becoming Ruby's friend. She seemed the sort of person Marti could trust, which meant she was dangerous. Because Marti knew Roger's secrets, and if there was anyone she could ever confide in…

Ruby sat down nearby, but not right beside her. She maintained a professional distance. It was almost as if she suspected how Marti was feeling. She'd tried to invite Marti out a few times before, but every time she'd suggested something – a quick coffee, or lunch, just the two of them – Marti was suddenly dragged back onto the campaign trail, or told to attend some private function.

Craig said it would be good for Marti's profile, that she'd get to meet influential people. But at its best, she maybe caught glimpses of such people.

At its worst…

Marti shook her head in disbelief. Friends and acquaintances thought it must be a dream to work for Roger ap Gwilliam. Other volunteers were jealous because she was part of his inner circle. Even her sister had been the subject of an online article that reported just how proud she was to see Marti finally making something of her life. And Marti knew she'd never be out of a job now. Roger couldn't risk her moving on.

'Good news,' Ruby lied, attempting small talk. Marti nodded in spite of herself, while all around them Roger's name filled the air, and his face leered down from every available surface.

'Between you and me,' said Ruby, 'I know he's brilliant, but sometimes I think…' She hesitated, as though suddenly nervous, looking around and deciding: 'He gives me the shivers.'

'Oh, he is a monster,' Marti confirmed with uneasy calmness.

Ruby said nothing. Instead, they heard Roger's laugh from every speaker. It was a laugh of joy and triumph, but also mockery. Like he alone knew the punchline to a joke he'd kept from everyone else in the country…

At least, from everyone except for Marti 'Boy's Name' Bridges.

Chapter 11
Cardiff

Roger ap Gwilliam was all about appearances. Even before his official victory was announced, his campaign team had been setting events in motion. Roger had grand plans, they all knew that much, and he spoke of a spectacular launch in the coming days. When that time came, where better to stage such an event than the city of Cardiff? If Albion's policies celebrated Britain's heritage and sense of identity, surely no statement was stronger than for the son of Wales to bring it back to his native country.

Of course, Cardiff wasn't his hometown – that was Swansea – but the capital made more sense, politically speaking. His campaign predicted that hundreds upon thousands would want to make the pilgrimage to see him, so a city with more reliable transport links was preferable.

They quickly secured the venue, at Roger's request: Cardiff City Stadium in Leckwith. Not the most glamorous of locations, perhaps, but still undeniably impressive.

Roger remembered going there as a child, once a month, to watch the Bluebirds play. His father always hoped he'd support Swansea City, but Cardiff felt much more exotic to a young lad like Roger. The stadium there could hold over 38,000 people, and when the home team scored a goal, the cheering would deafen him ... which was what Roger now hoped to achieve. Britain wanted to take back the world and so he would deafen this world with his nation's screams of joy.

It went without saying that his team could just have easily secured the larger Principality Stadium – the traditional venue for headliners visiting Cardiff, accommodating over twice the number of people – but Roger had humbly declined. He didn't want to risk appearing ostentatious, which was so *him*. In truth, however, he knew it had to be Cardiff City. His father always hated him for supporting the Bluebirds ... and Roger ap Gwilliam hated his father even more.

But the Cardiff of 2046 had little in common with the city he remembered. Gradually, over more than a decade, water levels had risen along the coast; the river

Taff had burst its banks and the Bay itself had flooded. A third of the city had been submerged by the threat of climate change.

Not that this bothered Roger. A private helicopter would take him where he needed to go, while his team would be housed in affordable hotels on the city's outskirts. The council would clear a route to the stadium, just as on match days, deploying pumps and sandbags to deal with the worst of it. Roger ap Gwilliam was going to put Cardiff back on the map. The cost to the country was trivial. Today, the world as they knew it would change for ever... and Roger's voice would be the only one that mattered.

Ruby had travelled up with the rest of her team in a convoy of coaches, which dropped them all off at a cheap hotel to the north of the city. Most of the staff from London had been dismissed, and those that remained had been thoroughly screened by Roger's security teams. Each floor was checked for listening devices and every room booked out. Nobody could enter or leave without authorisation.

In some ways, Ruby welcomed this. The very fact she was with them at all had to mean she was trusted, but she couldn't shake off her worry about being discovered.

* * *

The following day, a series of smaller shuttle buses transported the team from hotel to venue, escorted by a squad of police cars down through the city. When they arrived at the back of the stadium, their possessions were checked, in triplicate, by several security teams – first, the stadium's own private firm; then the police; and finally Roger's most trusted personal protection.

Nothing raised any alarm bells, as was expected, but the process was thorough. Bags and coats were scanned and pockets searched. Mobile devices were deemed essential for work but connectivity was blocked within the stadium itself, and all handsets would be checked again at the end of the day for any illicit recordings.

Satisfied, Craig led his personal group of volunteers from main reception down to the pitch. The route took them down a long and ominous tunnel, peppered with photos of previous glories. This was undoubtedly a venue with history, just as today's events would not be forgotten.

'We're here to help the PR team, okay?' Craig instructed in his most commanding voice. He carried with him an old-fashioned clipboard to denote that he was most definitely the one in charge. 'If you see anything suspect, talk to security – *and* back at the hotel. Eyes and ears open. We've got a busy three days ahead, so stay alert …'

Ruby found herself nodding along with everyone else in a desperate attempt to fit in, hoping the Woman's perception filter would keep her unnoticed in a space this size. But there was no absolute guarantee. All it took was for one person to ask the wrong question, or look the wrong way, and their cover was blown.

Sometimes Ruby thought that might be a relief, that perhaps someone might help her. But she'd made that mistake before. Worse, she wasn't sure who she could trust. She knew why *she'd* signed up to join Albion, but was never quite sure of the motives of others. Whenever she spoke with them one on one, their demeanour never chimed with Roger's rhetoric; but then, in situations like this, it was as if something altered – together, these people achieved a critical mass, and they were emboldened.

Everyone except Marti Bridges. Only she seemed as disturbed by this whole circus as Ruby was – and yet here she was, supporting Roger on his big day.

Ruby snorted softly. *It's what's expected of us*, she thought…

Ruby fell silent as she stepped out onto the pitch, dwarfed by the scale of the stadium. Seating snaked up and round them, row after row; massive screens and billboards that had once advertised holidays now shone with Gwilliam's name and the Albion slogan; and in huge white letters ahead of them, daubed proudly across the seats of the Ninian Stand, was the word *CARDIFF*.

As the group of volunteers emerged onto the sidelines, more security guards came forward, this time registering each of their lanyards on a portable scanner. This happened with monotonous regularity from sector to sector.

'If you could all be checked for clearance. Again!' Craig explained by way of apology. 'You know Roger. He arouses strong opinions.'

Bit of an understatement, thought Ruby, almost speaking the phrase out loud. But she bit her tongue and took in the spectacle.

Security guards and staff were stationed everywhere except the pitch, which was out of bounds. Some wore earpieces, some carried firearms – newly legalised by the Albion government – but each of them knew their function. Up by the Canton Stand, towards the north east, the goalposts had been removed. In their place stood workmen and a half-complete scaffold; when finished it would form the stage from which Roger would command his global audience.

Craig clapped his hands to get their attention. 'Rule number one,' he stated, raising his clipboard. 'Do *not* step on the grass.'

'I don't see why,' scoffed Akhim, one of the younger volunteers. 'Come Saturday, there's going to be 10,000 people standing on there!'

'And until then, keep off it,' Craig repeated more firmly. 'This place has a capacity for 40,000, plus 10,000 on the pitch. It's going to be amazing. Cardiff City, he's brought it home.' Craig gestured towards the semi-constructed stand. 'This place will broadcast Roger ap Gwilliam. All over the world!'

Ruby glanced back to the stage. It was already an impressive sight, elevated ten feet off the ground and flanked by two colossal display screens. But while everyone else was in awe of Gwilliam's pageantry, Ruby's attention was focused on a single figure, standing high up in the stands.

The Woman from Wales was back on home turf – and Ruby was happy.

'Here he is,' interrupted Marti, as a surge of distant movement distracted them.

Craig and the others watched as an important-looking entourage stormed the gates at the furthest end, flanking their leader.

He was hard to make out at first, but then the throng assumed their formal positions, allowing the man of the hour to be fully revealed.

Roger ap Gwilliam had officially arrived.

'Look at him,' gushed Akhim, as Roger cheerfully took the hand of every official, every bodyguard, every aide, and shook them vigorously. 'He still says hello to every single person. I'd love to meet him face to face.'

'Well, he's Prime Minister now,' replied Craig. 'We don't get access any more. Our job is just to stay on the sidelines.' Then he turned to face Marti, his thin smile barely concealing his resentment. 'Except for you, Marti. Roger said, there's room for you at the party on Saturday night. He even asked for you by name! Word is, it's going to be *wild*.'

He turned and walked away. 'Now, we need to help with the branding on the Grandstand,' he informed the rest of the team. 'Rows 11 to 61 …'

As Craig's voice receded into the distance, Ruby looked to Marti, clutching her arm in a silent promise. Marti nodded a tacit thanks and, together, they marched off to fulfil their duties.

The hours crept by slowly that day. The most important people flocked around Roger, busily conversing and choreographing, rehearsing for every and any eventuality. Roger ap Gwilliam was a man of the people – he had to look the part, which now meant appearing less polished and more spontaneous, none of which came naturally to him. Ruby supposed he must have spent a lifetime putting on a front, bottling up his feelings. She'd heard him describe himself as a coiled spring, ready for whatever life threw at him. But Ruby reckoned that if he could never relax, that was only because he'd lived a life ready to *run*.

Ruby was sitting with Craig and Marti, halfway up the Grandstand. Around them, a troop of more junior volunteers crossed slowly from row to row, affixing cheap vinyl Albion logos to the back of every seat. To Roger (and his party's anonymous donors), branding was everything.

With a flourish, Craig signed off Ruby's timesheets and handed them back to her. She'd done a good job, he told her, putting in all the hours, more so than the others. There was a bright future for people like her if they remained true.

Ruby sighed a noncommittal, 'Yeah,' and looked to the stage. Most of the scaffolding had now been concealed under red, white and blue, and technicians were busily working to connect the PA system. At regular intervals all around the stadium, oversized speakers were being erected and tested. Roger seemed determined to be heard no matter what. Ruby, however, was dubious.

'They won't be watching, though. The whole world,' she ventured aloud. 'Who cares about the British Prime Minister? Making a speech in Cardiff?'

'That's the point,' replied Craig. 'They'll listen. *If* he's got something to say...' He trailed off with a knowing smile.

'What d'you mean?'

'There are rumours,' he shrugged, turning his attention to the rest of his paperwork, reeling her in. 'They say... Saturday is when control transfers.'

'Control of what...?' Ruby asked, concerned.

Craig delighted in knowing more than anyone else. He put down his pen and papers, twisting in his chair to let Ruby in on his secret.

'We're purchasing the nuclear arsenal from Pakistan,' he grinned. 'And on Saturday, Roger will declare us independent from NATO. Saturday, Roger ap Gwilliam gets the codes!'

Ruby found she had nothing to say, there were no words. She stared across at Roger – that one lonely, angry little man, swamped in the middle of a stadium in the capital city, would soon have power over the entire planet. *So much* power.

Marti's face went white with dread. 'Saturday, he'll launch,' she told them both meekly.

'Don't be stupid, Marti!' Craig's voice was filled with venom. 'You're like those people on the Vine. It's symbolic! The moment is completely symbolic!'

Craig looked to Ruby for support but she was no longer listening.

She'd seen the same rumours online. Naysayers claiming that Roger ap Gwilliam was unfit for office, that he only wanted the power to govern the world. He had no real allies nor enemies, but that made everyone a viable target – and if Roger was one thing above all else, he was indiscriminate.

Somehow, in the pit of her stomach, Ruby knew: it was time now.

She looked across at Roger – one man with so much power, she almost couldn't believe it.

But that meant that she had power too.

As Craig returned to his work, Ruby rose from her seat and turned to Marti. This moment was long overdue, and even though she didn't know what would happen next, this might be her only opportunity. She couldn't sit back any longer.

'I'm sorry I took so long,' she told Marti kindly. 'Because I think I'll only get one chance. And I had to make sure I was right. But I wish I could have helped you. I'm so sorry.'

Before Marti could ask any questions, Ruby took a deep breath and turned away. There was no looking back. Slowly, she considered every step, crossing to the end of the row and then down each step, closer and closer to the pitch.

The movement caught Craig's attention. 'Get us a coffee while you're there!' he yelled.

But Ruby didn't reply. Instead, she kept walking with increased purpose, quickly picking up speed. She knew what she had to do now – in fact, she'd never been more certain in her life. Calmly, she kept on moving, head held high … over the sidelines and onto the pitch.

At first, no one paid much attention. There were so many different bodies dotted about, everyone intent on keeping busy. Besides, Ruby was just one woman, no one important.

Then Craig must've clocked her. 'Ruby!' he yelled. 'I said, keep off the grass!'

But she kept walking, slowly and surely, out towards the centre of the pitch. With every step, she felt her heels digging into the soft green grass of the field.

She thought she might be getting away with it. But Craig's outburst had managed to attract the groundsman's attention, prompting a chain of angry reactions.

'Hey, get off the pitch, love!' barked the groundsman – but Ruby pretended not to hear and kept on walking. One of the security officers, halfway down the sidelines, turned to see what was going on.

'Ruby,' Craig demanded, 'what are you doing?'

Ruby didn't look back, not once, but she could feel each one of them looking. All eyes were turning to watch her now, including Roger ap Gwilliam's. Her political life was over, she knew that for certain. As for what the rest of her life had in store, she couldn't even begin to imagine.

If I don't do this, Ruby thought, *then there is no rest of my life*.

She reached the centre of the pitch and stopped walking, then she looked up directly at Roger.

Roger stared back at Ruby from his position high up on the podium. 'What's she doing?' he asked an aide, but nobody on his team could explain what was happening.

At the back of his mind, Roger recognised Ruby from somewhere. He'd seen her before, on his campaign.

A volunteer, no one important. And if she thought it made sense to hijack his big day, she'd quickly learn what a man like him was truly capable of.

If she wasn't careful, nobody would see or hear from her ever again.

But Ruby saw Roger.

Reaching into the pocket of her sheepskin coat, she drew out her phone and held it in front of her. She activated the camera and – *snap!* – she took a photo.

'There's no unofficial photographs, thank you!' a distant aide screeched at her helplessly.

Ruby couldn't help but smile as she kept the camera app open. The image was now live on her phone and its statistics were active. As the lenses fought to find their focus, the phone's display updated its distance from the highlighted object, second by second, calibrated to Ruby's personal preferences.

55 yards, it announced, capturing Roger in its sights … completely missing the Woman on the stand a few rows behind him.

It wasn't enough, not yet. So Ruby began to walk backwards.

56 yards, 57 yards …

* * *

Craig got up from his seat. He'd never live this down at HQ. 'Ruby!' he shouted, loud as he could. He hoped that she might listen to him at least. 'Just stop it and come back here! Ruby!'

61 yards, 62...

Ruby looked down at her screen.

'I said, get off the pitch!' It was the groundsman again. 'Are you listening? Get off the pitch!'

'Hey! Could you get off the grass?' There was a security guard to her right now, rushing up to join an armed policeman. The latter carried a belt-fed light machine gun; Roger aroused strong opinions, after all.

67 yards, 68...

'I will have to ask you to put down that device immediately!' snapped the security guard. The policeman, sensing danger, readied his weapon.

But Ruby carried on backing away. She'd been driven this far already. What did she have left to lose?

From her seat at the back of the Grandstand, Marti Bridges started to grin. She didn't know what or why, but something was happening. Everyone felt it.

'Ruby!' Craig was still yelling. 'Stop it! Ruby!'

* * *

70 yards, 71…

The armed policeman hoisted up his gun, levelling it directly at Ruby. 'Stay where you are!' he instructed, 'that's an order.'

But Ruby refused to comply. She was almost where she needed to be.

'I said, stay where you are!'

More armed police moved to join him, raising their firearms. A security guard aimed his pistol, sensing the mood.

All eyes were on Ruby Sunday…

Which was exactly what she wanted. Because it meant that none of them could see what was coming next.

72 yards…

And with a deep breath, Ruby took –

one

    more

        step.

73 yards.

'Final warning!' screamed the policeman. 'Stay! Where! You! Are!'

At last, Ruby lowered the phone.

'That's exactly what I'm going to do,' she said with a smile.

Looking up, she saw Roger glaring at her – his meticulously composed expression had now given way to one of simmering fury. He turned to ask one of his aides to have Ruby removed, but then suddenly flinched.

There was an old woman standing next to him.

Instinctively, Roger thought he should apologise for not seeing her, even though it was clearly the woman's fault. But then, looking at her, he realised... this stranger wasn't one of his team, she had no lanyard... and yet here she was, presuming to share the stage with the most powerful man on the planet. She seemed to be speaking too, but ever so softly.

Was this some kind of protest? Like the other woman, standing on the pitch.

Roger struggled to make out the newcomer's words, even though they were barely any distance apart. She was repeating a peculiar gesture – tilting her head and rubbing her palms – but there was nothing in her hands. She wasn't a threat.

So why did he feel so uneasy?

All eyes in the stadium were on the newly elected Prime Minister.

Roger stepped forward, leaning in to hear what the Woman was saying.

As she spoke, the Woman continued to shrug and rub her palms.

Oddly, she was always looking forward – never at Roger, but always at the woman on the pitch.

Ruby watched with dread and excitement as Roger turned to face her too. The expression he wore, she knew so well. It was the look she'd been given by Carla all those years ago, twisted in horror and hatred. But unlike Carla, Roger had done so much wrong in the world, abused his power, covered up the worst of atrocities. Whatever the Woman had told him, it couldn't be worse than those … could it?

Ruby held his gaze as the air grew heavy and held her breath.

Roger looked as though he were staring into hell.

Suddenly he turned and ran from the stage. *Sprinted.*

The Prime Minister fleeing from the site of his triumph.

Roger hauled himself onto the handrail, at the top of the stage, then jumped down onto the ground, pushing past aides and police.

He was like a wild animal trapped in a cage, desperate and terrified, hunting feverishly for any means of escape.

The panic was contagious.

All of a sudden, a decision was made. Ruby no longer mattered – everyone else cared solely about Roger, and something had spooked him.

If anyone saw the Woman, nobody noticed her.

Instead, assistants ran competitively after Gwilliam, urging him back, each hoping to be the one that talked him down. The security guards sensed this hysteria and set off in pursuit with the armed policemen. Roger raced down one of the tunnels, chased by police and colleagues, screaming all the while for an exit.

Nobody had ever glimpsed this side to Roger ap Gwilliam. He'd lost all sense of swagger, his confidence stolen; now he was just a man like all the rest of them.

Roger spotted an emergency exit and stormed past a film crew, shoving the cameraman roughly to one side. Quickly, the crew grabbed their equipment, and though the footage they caught was fleeting, it captured the tension in that moment.

A second later, Roger broke free and calm ensued.

It was almost as if all the world's troubles were running away with him.

* * *

Ruby now stood alone at the heart of the stadium. So many victories had been won here, but she felt that this might be the greatest of them all. She turned to Marti who was laughing delightedly, tears coursing down her cheeks.

Unnoticed in all the chaos, the Woman endured. Was it over now, wondered Ruby, had they finally done it? The Woman's expression remained indifferent.

Sorry, she shrugged, the same shrug for over two decades. *Sorry. Sorry. Sorry.*

But none of that mattered right now.

Breaking into a run, Ruby crossed the pitch to Marti Bridges ...

Chapter 12
The Aftermath

The country had been thrown into chaos. But following Roger's flight from Cardiff City Stadium, political parties had rallied. The Opposition called for an immediate halt to Gwilliam's more controversial policies – including his plans for mandatory DNA testing throughout the United Kingdom – while Deputy Prime Minister Iris Cabriola took control of the party.

She promised Britain 'a more lenient and listening government'.

Roger ap Gwilliam's downfall was welcomed across the globe. In Washington, for instance, President Matarazzo issued a statement expressing his 'joy and delight' at Gwilliam's departure. In a world that felt fractured by anger day after day, this was a rare instance of shared positivity.

Ruby watched from her sofa as Roger's vapid publicity photo flashed up on the news, accompanied by the soothing voice of its evening newscaster.

'...and 50 minutes later, Roger ap Gwilliam resigned from the office of Prime Minister, refusing to give any reason for his actions.'

The screen cut from the former Prime Minister's portrait to a more dishevelled image of Roger. He was still dressed in his suit from earlier, framed in the door of his West London townhouse, desperately trying to deal with a crowd of reporters. His eyes boggled with wild alarm as they kept repeating the very same question:

But why did you resign? Why...? Why...? Why...?

Roger looked down the lens of one camera. 'Ask her,' he said. Then another. 'Ask her,' he repeated, more angrily. Then he yelled to whoever might listen, one final time – '*Ask her!*' – and slammed the door.

From her sofa, Ruby raised a glass of warm champagne. To Roger ap Gwilliam! And to the Woman who made all this happen.

With a sip, she moved to the window, looking out across the city. It had changed so much in the last 20 years. London's horizon rose and fell, but mostly rose, and you could barely see the stars for all the skyscrapers.

Even now, standing proud above the capital, she could see what remained of UNIT Tower. But it had long since been abandoned.

With the Doctor gone, and time itself 'suspended' along this event, there were no threats to the human race; at least, not from anything extraterrestrial. On any passing day, UNIT might previously have detected several alien signatures passing through the Milky Way... but now there was nothing. Reports of the supernatural had dwindled; the number of paranormal podcasts diminished; and for the first time since it was established after the Underground Incident back in the nineteen-whatevers, UNIT had no real remit.

When Kate Lethbridge-Stewart chose to take early retirement, the Unified Intelligence Taskforce retired with her. What technology they'd been able to scavenge was surrendered to the appropriate departments within Britain's government, and the extraterrestrial 'guests' they had held in containment cells were 'euthanised'.

The grand old UNIT Tower, which had once been such a beacon of hope on London's skyline, soon became a husk of empty corridors and dusty old conference rooms – but also, a developer's dream. The Unit, as it was later rebranded, boasted a vast array of restaurants and cafés on its lower levels, with shopping arcades just above them, and a wealth of unaffordable housing all the way up to its summit. The views, so the brochure claimed, were second to none, and the penthouse apartment came with its own private helipad.

None of the residents would ever know what had truly happened there, or how close the world had come to ending within those walls. Instead, they were glad of their inner-city parking concessions, and free access to the Unit's gymnasium.

Only the concierge, Osgood, seemed to know what the Unit had been, but since she'd signed the Official Secrets Act, she'd never let on.

Instead, she spent the rest of her life there, waiting and hoping... because she would never give up on the Doctor, even if everyone else had.

But the Doctor was gone now, truly – and eventually, after decades of service to UNIT in all its forms, so would she be.

Ruby's eyes flicked down to the courtyard where the Woman from Wales looked back at her, shrugging her shoulders, 73 yards away.

They were still reporting Roger's resignation on the news.

'Is that it?' Ruby quietly wondered, under her breath. 'Is that what you were for? Can you leave me alone now?'

She wasn't expecting an answer, but at the back of her mind she dared to hope that something had changed – that the timelines were resetting; that she might blink and the Woman would vanish. Maybe she'd even hear the groan of the TARDIS engines?

That night, Ruby Sunday went to bed with hope in her heart, and her eyes closed almost as soon as her head hit the pillow.

It was the first night she'd slept properly in 22 years.

The circumstances surrounding Roger's resignation instantly captured the public's imagination. No one truly knew what had happened inside that stadium. Conspiracy theories sprang up about an old woman who'd evaded security. Some people insisted it was a plot by foreign powers. Others simply claimed that Roger had 'bottled it'. But a raft of non-disclosure agreements and security processes meant that nobody could ever be truly sure who had been present that day.

An unnamed source mentioned Ruby to one of the tabloids. 'Moody Ruby,' they called her. The term followed the story around like its very own ghost.

People even made documentaries about it (although not very good ones).

It was close to a decade before Roger chose to break his silence. He claimed it was because 'at last, the people have a right to know what happened'. In truth, it was down to a lucrative book deal hastily arranged in the wake of a long-overdue divorce. In what the publishers asserted were 'his story, his words', Roger made claims of a significant threat against him, but always refused to comment when people pressed further. To say any more, he suggested, would be to reignite the fire under his enemies.

The book topped the nonfiction bestseller charts for almost two weeks, then Roger ap Gwilliam faded back into welcome obscurity.

His career had ended in much the same way it had begun: with a lie.

Chapter 13
The TARDIS

9 November 2086

Forty years had passed since Roger ap Gwilliam stood down as Prime Minister. He'd held office for less than a month but enjoyed all its pensions and privileges for the rest of his life … a life that had ended abruptly, the day before his 50th birthday. Barely anyone attended the funeral. The cause of death remained undisclosed, though the few friends who had remained in Roger's orbit were aware of his struggles. He had been haunted by his past, the mistakes he'd made, incapable of ever saying sorry. Now, he was just an unpleasant, forgotten footnote in British politics.

Not that the Britain that Roger had fought for existed any more. The political landscape had altered, even if the physical landscape remained very much the same.

As temperatures across the planet rose, some coastal villages crumbled beneath the waves; but on the cliffs not far from a sleepy Welsh town called Glyngatwyg, life seemed to endure in some kind of stasis.

Very few people went up there. It was a place that was long forgotten by most, though some still remembered. An old police box – defunct and covered in lichen – acted like a beacon for geocachers and hikers alike. It remained one of the most serenely still places on Earth … and almost nobody knew of it.

The rhythmic crash of the waves was interrupted by the spluttering of an engine, as a battered old muddy jeep attempted an incline on a nearby dirt track. Its wheels spun round and round hopelessly until its progress was halted. Then the driver-side door sprang open and out hopped Elizabeth.

Ruby Sunday hadn't known Elizabeth that long. She was one of the newer carers in Ruby's retirement home, only recently qualified, but full of warmth and optimism. Ruby admired that more than anything. She remembered when she was young and people despaired for the state of the planet. The world never wanted to listen and yet it survived – it always would – as long as there were people out there like Elizabeth who wanted to care for it.

'I'm sorry, Ruby, I can't drive any closer,' Elizabeth said, pulling open the passenger door. She surveyed a rusting aerial on the vehicle's roof. 'I can't get a signal for the engine, this far out.'

'No, it's fine,' smiled Ruby, helping herself down from the jeep with her most trusted cane. She'd wrapped up warm – turtleneck sweater and tartan jacket – remembering her very first time there, though the weather was surprisingly balmy for November.

Elizabeth guided the old woman along by the elbow, helping Ruby steady herself on the terrain.

'I haven't been here in such a long time.' Ruby told her, breathing in deep. The place somehow smelled the same; free of all the smog and pollution the world had grown so accustomed to. Across the clifftops, she spotted the familiar silhouette of the TARDIS. It had seemed so strange and alien when she was just 19 years old; now it was suddenly the most familiar thing in the world.

Ruby beamed. 'What a beautiful view.'

Elizabeth looked round and nodded, unaware that – while Ruby surveyed the police box – an even older Woman was surveying them as well. But Elizabeth could be forgiven for not noticing.

That Woman was 73 yards behind them, after all.

* * *

With Elizabeth by her side, Ruby slowly stumbled across to where the TARDIS stood and laid a small bunch of roses on the ground at the foot of the door. Similar offerings were scattered all around; some of the petals had withered, some were just stalks, but it was a sign that the space was still important. People *cared*.

The Fairy Circle that had kicked off this chain of events – if that was indeed the case – now extended proudly around the police box base. Strands of cotton stretched around its framework, supporting a raft of mementoes and memories. Some had been there for over 60 years while others were far more recent additions.

One message, bleached by sunlight, caught Ruby's attention. The writing was stained and faded, but the sentiment was legible even after so many years. *Love you, Josh*, it read. Ruby even recognised the handwriting from the hastily scribbled bill that Lowri confronted her with, back at Y Pren Marw ... a lifetime ago now.

She'd never found out what happened to them. Until that moment, they had been almost like ghosts. A distant memory haunting her. Days so awful, she longed to forget. And yet, now she was here, 62 years on, and it seemed almost like yesterday.

She hoped, at the very least, that Ifor was happy.

'Why do people put flowers here?' Elizabeth asked.

'I don't think they know,' replied Ruby.

The country was steeped in blood, or so she'd been told. (*Poor Enid*, Ruby thought; she'd be gone now too.) Of course, they could have made some of them up – the Spiteful One, Mad Jack – but there were so many *more*. The Lady of the Lake, Mari Lwyd, Twm Siôn Cati, not to mention everything in the Mabinogion; Ruby had read up on them all. And however far-fetched and fantastical each might seem, Ruby knew in her heart that each was grounded in truth. Just as the tales that surrounded the TARDIS were grounded in hers.

Ruby shed a tear for that daft old police box. It had shone with so much life once, inside and out. Now, the shell was hollow, shrouded in moss and dew-soaked cobwebs. People had carved crude graffiti into the woodwork, and flakes of paintwork drifted off on the cruel sea breeze.

Pretending not to notice the old woman's tears, Elizabeth helped settle Ruby into a camping chair, wrapped her up beneath a blanket and returned to the jeep until she was called for.

Now was the time for Ruby to spend with her memories, to make peace with her past.

At her age, she knew better than anyone not to

take it for granted. It had been a good many years since she'd last made it up here, and somehow she knew that this would be the final time.

The Woman dressed in black shrugged her age-old apology and Ruby Sunday was happy. Once, she'd wanted nothing more than to never see that Woman again. Now, with each passing year, the Woman's familiar presence provided her comfort. Especially here, back where it all began.

What a beautiful view, Ruby thought.

Ten minutes passed… ten minutes of peaceful contemplation. Ruby even found the crash of the waves relaxing. The chaos of nature was wholly unpredictable, and completely at odds with the patterns of life that she'd fallen into.

'… and the drought gets worse,' she explained, addressing her words (apparently) to the TARDIS. 'We're allowed a shower for 30 seconds, once a week. 30 seconds and it cuts off – that's not a shower, it's a splash.' Ruby rolled her eyes. 'It's become a funny old world, Doctor. And a stinky one!'

Ruby allowed herself the smallest of laughs, then looked at the police box windows. The sunlight momentarily seemed to bring them back to life. Ruby missed the Doctor more than ever now. She'd had to say goodbye to so many people over the years: those she'd loved and lost … and those she never really got to know in the first place.

'I presume she must be gone, my mother,' Ruby continued, still haunted by the look on Carla's face. 'No one ever told me. And I didn't find my birth mother. It never snowed again. But I keep thinking …' She rallied herself from her camping chair. 'I know why.'

She looked across at the figure 73 yards away.

'The Woman. I've been thinking about it my whole life. Why she's here. And I think, at the end, I have hope.' Ruby's eyes were welling up now. 'Because that's very you, isn't it? My dear old friend.'

She looked at that bigger-on-the-inside police box, one last time.

'I dare to *hope* …'

Chapter 14
The Woman

Five years later, Ruby Sunday was 86 years old.

The world had changed so much since she was left on the steps outside the church on Ruby Road. She'd changed more than she could ever have imagined. In her head, she thanked the Doctor for that... wherever he might be.

'This timeline might be suspended along your event.'

Ruby had never been entirely certain what that meant. She'd had her suspicions, of course, but the only people who could have confirmed those ideas had run away from her and never looked back.

Ruby was used to that now.

All her life, she'd lost people. Her family had abandoned her, her friends had mostly settled and drifted away, and any hint of real romance had pretty much passed her by.

As a result, Ruby never spent much of her savings – she was always far more generous with others than herself, but there were never that many others to start with – meaning she was able to spend her final days in a cosy little nursing home on the outskirts of Manchester. It was a nice enough space, Ruby thought, and she had her own room. Everything was a soothing combination of blue and white pastels (even Ruby's pyjamas), though she had persuaded the nurses to bring her a plant: a single concession to their otherwise neutral colour scheme.

The nurses themselves were friendly, though it took a while to remember their names. It had been so long since she'd had to remember *anyone's* name. She'd become so accustomed to losing people, she never realised how much she kept herself apart.

But now, in her final days, she allowed herself to grow close to others again, while her enigmatic companion remained somewhere, out of sight, 73 yards away.

Ruby was no longer bothered who might see, or who might listen.

Tonight, there was a new nurse on duty. She popped her head in just before bedtime to give Ruby her tablets and make sure she was comfortable. Her smile lit up the room, though the curtains were drawn, and she sat with Ruby for longer than she probably ought to. It was a habit they'd fallen into. All the staff had commented on how Ruby never had visitors, so each of them would spare a few moments here or there, that extra bit of time to make her feel special.

'I've set the light, Ruby,' she said, still with that smile. 'If you wake you in the night, you say, "Light" out loud, and it comes on.'

Ruby sighed. 'Yes, I know, that's not new. We had that when *I* was young.'

The nurse stifled a laugh and tugged at her tunic, ready to leave. 'Anything else you need?'

Ruby considered for a moment. She hadn't needed anything for so many years. Her life may not have been easy, but it had been good – it had been *hers* – and she'd never let anything defeat her.

But then a random thought suddenly struck her: 'I could make it snow. Once upon a time.'

'That's nice,' said the nurse, rising to her feet. She seemed almost apologetic. 'If you need me, I'm just down the hall. So you won't be on your own.'

'Don't worry,' Ruby assured her. 'Everyone has abandoned me, my whole life. But I haven't been alone for 67 years.'

The nurse offered another smile, unsure what to say. 'Night then, Ruby,' she added, followed by a slightly more commanding, 'Light off!'

And everything dissolved into darkness ...

Hours passed. Ruby remained shrouded in shadow until she was woken by the strangest sound: a whisper in her ears, the crashing of waves.

Startled, she sat upright in her bed, her eyes flicking open. She clutched at her bedsheets for comfort but they felt suddenly harsh and heavy, almost like hessian, coarse against her fragile, wrinkled skin. The atmosphere in the room – that once safe, clinical atmosphere – had now changed. She took a single deep breath to steady herself, but as the cold air filled her nostrils, she realised that that had changed too, the sterile stench of disinfectant replaced by the ancient timeless scent of briny seas.

The crashing of waves grew louder.

Those whispers ... like a *warning*.

'Light!' Ruby cried; she was sure she wasn't alone now. And in the faintest of glows as her bedside lamp illuminated, her suspicion was quickly confirmed.

For the first time in over six decades, the Woman was with her.

In the room.

The Woman stood solemnly in one corner, her face turned away.

Ruby pushed herself up on her elbows, rising to face the Woman. She might have wondered how this was happening, why the Woman had come to her – but in her heavily beating heart, she already knew.

As Ruby's heart began to falter, so did the bedside lamp. She felt the darkness creeping steadily closer, swallowing up the light. And yet the Woman was always visible – standing in front of her, dressed in black – just as Ruby had always seen her.

The crashing of waves grew louder as the air became heavier. Ruby could feel the pressure building around her. Something was happening, *everything* was changing. The entire world was turning around this moment, Ruby could feel it. The roar of the sea, the crashing of timelines; so many voices whispering in her mind. If history had indeed been suspended somehow, then this was its breaking point.

Suddenly, silence fell. But more than an absence of sound, this was something greater.

A moment of purity.

Chaos had been and gone, and now peace was being slowly restored.

Ruby looked to the Woman for answers but saw only shadow. Tears obscured her vision as the lights continued to flicker, occasionally flaring; with each abrupt flash of darkness, it almost seemed as if the Woman was drawing closer … halfway across the room. Then the lamplight faltered again, plunging Ruby into darkness, bringing the Woman closer still – to the end of her bed now. Her silhouette seemed somehow more defined – that bombazine dress, white hair – but her face remained concealed …

Until the lights began to tremble, fluttering in and out of shadow, coaxing the Woman into action after so many years.

Ruby watched as the shape at the end of her bed began to turn, imperceptibly at first but then more deliberately. Ruby reached out her arms imploringly, greeting the Woman after so many years, embracing what was to come. She had never been so afraid, nor so full of hope.

As she raised her arms to the Woman, one final time, Ruby's whole life flashed before her. She remembered it all. Every nurse who had come to care for her. Each misjudged boyfriend. The workmates who were always so patient. People who drifted in and out of her life, just as she'd drifted into and out of theirs …

Then there was Roger ap Gwilliam, the Prime Minister she'd destroyed.

Carla and Cherry Sunday who'd taken her in and shown so much love.

Abdul, Mrs Flood and the rest of her neighbours.

Trudy and her bandmates, Clark and Big Jim.

Shobna and Bex and Suleen.

The Doctor, of course.

And Marti. The one person she'd always said she would never forget.

For decades, Ruby Sunday had wondered what this Woman could have said to drive so many people away. And now, as the pressure reached breaking point, she finally heard the Woman's words. They were indistinct – syllables tumbling to form secrets that should never be shared, whispering like a voice from an open grave – but she understood ... and she forgave them, each and every one of them. Carla most of all.

And in that same instant, the Woman's awful forbidden words stopped Ruby's heart.

Chapter 15
The End

Ruby Sunday died alone in a nursing home in 2091...

And, at the very same moment, Ruby Sunday was also reborn. On 9 November 2024.

As Ruby blinked, for what she believed would be the very last time, she looked up to see a dazzling autumn sky. The daylight was almost blinding, and yet... she remembered it all so clearly. Those clouds, hanging heavy above her. The tang of salt in the air. The buffeting winds. Even that gnarled old tree with its twisted branches stripped of all their leaves.

This was where the Doctor had left her, all those years ago. And now she was back, her old arms reaching out.

I'm sorry, she said. *I'm sorry, I'm sorry...*

Because Ruby Sunday knew what was coming next.

She'd never seen it happen before – she'd always been on the inside – but far across the clifftops, she saw a familiar blue police box fade into view, accompanied by a joyful cacophony of temporal engines.

The last time she'd seen the TARDIS, it had been abandoned, overgrown by years of weeds and moss – but now it looked exactly as she always remembered it, in her heart. 67 years undone in the blink of an eye: the magic of time travel.

I'm sorry I took so long, she felt herself say. *I tried and I tried. I tried so hard. What else could I do? It took all these years.*

All these long years.

The doors of the TARDIS snapped open, and out stepped the Doctor.

'Yes!' he cheered excitedly. 'Spectacular! We are in Wales!'

And look at me, the older Ruby thought. *I was so young…*

She watched as her younger self quickly moved to follow the Doctor, shutting the doors to the TARDIS behind them. 'How can you tell?' asked young Ruby, bracing herself against the icy coastal air.

The Doctor, however, embraced it, throwing his arms out wide.

'That smell,' he beamed, gesturing round their surroundings. 'That green. That coastline, Ruby! The rocks and the water, it never ends. The war between the land and the sea.'

Ruby followed him as he marched towards some farmland.

'I've been to Wales three times,' she said. 'I went to see Shygirl in Cardiff. Then I went to the Mumbles, when I was 16, because of a boy. I think I broke his heart, but there you go.'

'Oh, bless him.' The Doctor kept moving forward. 'Mind you, Roger ap Gwilliam. That's a bad example of the Welsh. Terrifying!' He clapped his hands to reinforce the point. 'The most dangerous Prime Minister in history...'

Don't step.

Ruby paused – did she just hear something? Then she noticed a figure on the horizon.

'Who's she?' Ruby asked.

The Doctor turned. 'Who?'

Then that voice again, so faint and yet so firm. *Don't step.*

'Over there!' Ruby insisted, pointing towards the distant woman. She seemed to be gesturing.

'Where …?' the Doctor asked, searching.

Don't step.

They both looked back, but the Woman was no longer visible. The only thing that stood out was a strange old withered tree, approximately 73 yards from where they were standing.

Ruby inspected the scene. 'There was a woman.'

'Not any more.'

'No, but there *was* a woman, she was standing over there.' Ruby glanced round. 'Maybe she was looking for someone?'

The Doctor leapt forward—

'Oh, no no no no no no, don't step!' Ruby moved fast and grabbed the Doctor, pulling him back to her. Together, they noticed the ground beneath their feet: strands of cotton looped to form a large, elaborate circle – roughly seven feet in diameter – decorated with all manner of mementoes and keepsakes.

'Oh, I almost broke that,' realised the Doctor, kneeling beside it, and Ruby knelt next to him. 'Careful,' he added, studying the various trinkets. 'Oh, honey, what a beautiful thing.'

Ruby examined the circle of string: the knots and the love-hearts, pegs and scrolls … even the tiny bird skulls. 'What is it?'

'Some kind of Fairy Circle.' The Doctor smiled. 'Man, that is so delicate. Charms and spells and wishes and hopes and *dreams*. Here at the end of the land.'

'What do they say?'

Ruby was about to reach for a scroll but the Doctor stopped her.

'No, better not. Give them respect, Ruby. Let them rest in peace.' He glanced back to where Ruby had pointed. 'Like your mysterious woman.'

'Oh, she *was* there,' Ruby laughed.

'And we,' said the Doctor, grinning, 'are here!'

Springing to his feet, the Doctor carefully negotiated his way round the circle, striding back the way they'd come.

'So what was the third time?' asked the Doctor, descending a ridge. 'You said you'd been to Wales three times. What was the other one?'

'Oh, that was, um ... I can't think. When was it?'

Ruby paused. She'd never been here before and yet it felt so familiar.

She shrugged the sensation off. 'I don't know, I suppose it must've been ... *now*.'

And as she looked back across the scrubland, Ruby saw that gnarled old tree standing proud against the horizon.

It had survived this long, she thought, enduring in an unpredictable world and weathering whatever the elements threw at it.

And somehow, Ruby knew how that must feel.

She always would.

Acknowledgements

It's been an absolute delight to revisit *73 Yards* for this novelisation, a year and a half after the script first landed in my inbox (giving me chills on a hot summer's day).

Like the show itself, there are a huge number of people to thank – some more involved than others – but each important in wildly different ways.

First of all, I'd like to thank the team at BBC Books for their guidance and trust throughout the whole process: Steve Cole and Shammah Banerjee in particular; but also James Page at BBC Studios; and the trio of former novelisers James Goss, Pete McTighe and Gary Russell, all of whom offered as much gossip and caffeine as they ever did advice.

Thanks to Lawrence Blunt, Emily Cook, Jacob Dudman, Sean Longmore, Blair Mowat and Jonny Thomas for keeping me sane away from the

Whoniverse – and to everyone involved in *Tales of the TARDIS*, which proved the most delightful reason to agree an extension.

Most of all, however, this book would be nothing without the incredible team at *Doctor Who* – not just Ncuti, Millie and the rest of the cast, but the entire Wolf Pack. Special mentions go to Jonathon Aiken, Shane Crowley, Dee Brooker, Adam Byard, Abdoul Razak Ceesay, Laura Gardner, Chris Harkus, Lauren Pate, Ariana Scott and Mikey Williams for all the adventures away from studio; Rasheed Bello, Ellen Marsh and Joshua Thomas for being my '*semperdistans*' office companions; and executive producers Jane Tranter, Julie Gardner, Joel Collins and Phil Collinson for inspiring such a brilliant group of people (and inviting me along for the ride).

As for *73 Yards* itself, so much of the episode's success is down to the combined powers of producer Vicki Delow, 1st assistant director Geraint Havard Jones, director of photography Sam Care and of course director Dylan Holmes Williams. And to everyone on that Pembrokeshire recce – we survived!

But none of us would be here, watching the episode or reading the book, without the creative force of nature that is Russell T Davies.

It's been a pleasure to work so hard alongside so many friends.

Finally, to the most important friend of all: Tim Leng, thank you for everything.

Also available in the Target series from BBC Books

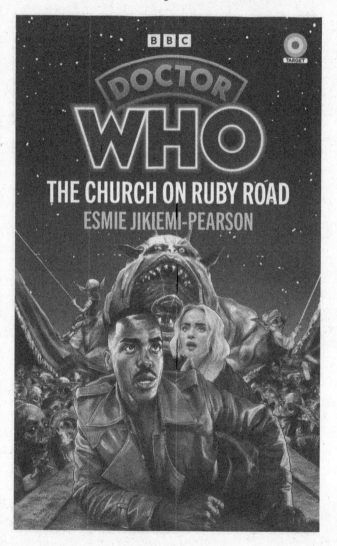

BBC

TARGET

DOCTOR
WHO

THE CHURCH ON RUBY ROAD

ESMIE JIKIEMI-PEARSON

ROGUE

KATE HERRON &
BRIONY REDMAN

Also available from BBC Books

BBC

DOCTOR WHO

POLICE BOX

RUBY
RED

GEORGIA COOK

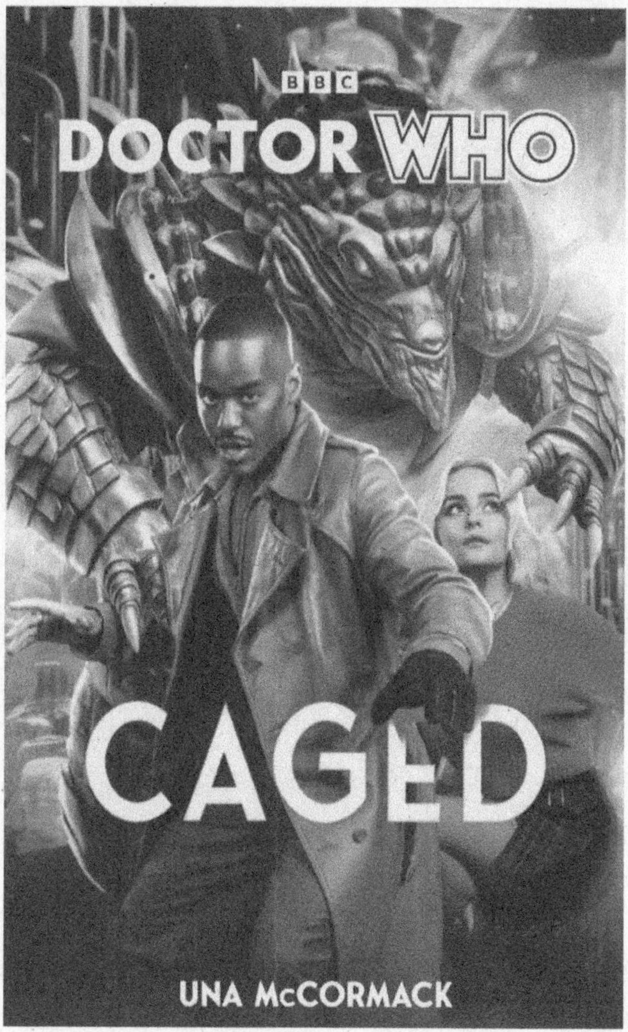
BBC
DOCTOR WHO
CAGED
UNA McCORMACK